Robert Riddell

Mechanics' Geometry

plainly teaching the carpenter, joiner, mason, metal-plate worker, in fact the

artisan in any and every branch of industry whatsoever, the constructive principles

of his calling

Robert Riddell

Mechanics' Geometry
plainly teaching the carpenter, joiner, mason, metal-plate worker, in fact the artisan in any and every branch of industry whatsoever, the constructive principles of his calling

ISBN/EAN: 9783337381820

Printed in Europe, USA, Canada, Australia, Japan

Cover: Foto ©Andreas Hilbeck / pixelio.de

More available books at **www.hansebooks.com**

MECHANICS' GEOMETRY,

PLAINLY TEACHING THE

CARPENTER, JOINER, MASON, METAL-PLATE WORKER,

IN FACT THE

ARTISAN

IN ANY AND EVERY BRANCH OF INDUSTRY WHATSOEVER,

THE CONSTRUCTIVE PRINCIPLES OF HIS CALLING.

Illustrated by

ACCURATE EXPLANATORY CARD-BOARD MODELS AND DIAGRAMS.

BY

ROBERT RIDDELL,

Author of "Hand-Railing Simplified," "Practical Geometry," "The Carpenter and Joiner," Etc.

PREFACE.

THE book here presented to the public is intended to serve the double purpose of aiding the student — whether he be man or boy — in understanding the theory of geometry, and of giving the boy who is about to choose a trade a clear idea of the geometric principles upon which much of his future work will be based. To secure these ends, the illustrations that have been used are not mere surface pictures, requiring the use of the imagination to present them to the mind, but they are, at the same time, surface pictures and plane models.

Illustrations can only be read and comprehended by minds that have been educated in the language they use to convey thought to the mind. To a geometrician, a few lines drawn on a flat surface will express that which can be shown to the novice only by means of blocks and of careful drawings. In this book the language of illustration is one that can be comprehended by all minds: it is the language of form, of visible presences. The student can see the lines brought together in actual projection, and can then more readily understand the geometric plan the parts will cover when laid back upon the level surface of the illustration.

An elementary work that impresses so forcibly the practical value of the rules it is designed to teach, will interest the student and afford him excellent mental training, without overtasking the mind by mere memorizing.

To the boy about to learn a trade of which geometry is an underlying principle, that which is otherwise dry, and, to the boy-mind, barren of fruit, becomes in this book an attractive study. He can see for himself its advantages, his ambition will be aroused, and he will labor with that feeling without which good results are seldom obtained — the feeling of personal pleasure.

It will also be found useful, though possibly in a less degree, to those who have already become mechanics, but who have not learned the science involved in their trade.

So much of the prosperity of any community depends upon the skill of its workmen, whatever may be its natural wealth of resources, that the education of mechanics in the science of their trade becomes a matter of national importance. It is believed that this treatise will do something towards increasing the skill of American mechanics, besides stimulating the minds of boys who desire to excel in some of the more intricate branches of human labor. If it should make but a few of our working-people *master* mechanics, in the true sense of that term, it will have incidentally solved some of the social problems of the day with regard to labor, and will have met, in some degree, the wishes of the author.

ROBERT RIDDELL,
1214 HANCOCK STREET,
PHILADELPHIA, 1874.

3

Perpendicular, Horizontal and Oblique.

Forces.

Plate 1.

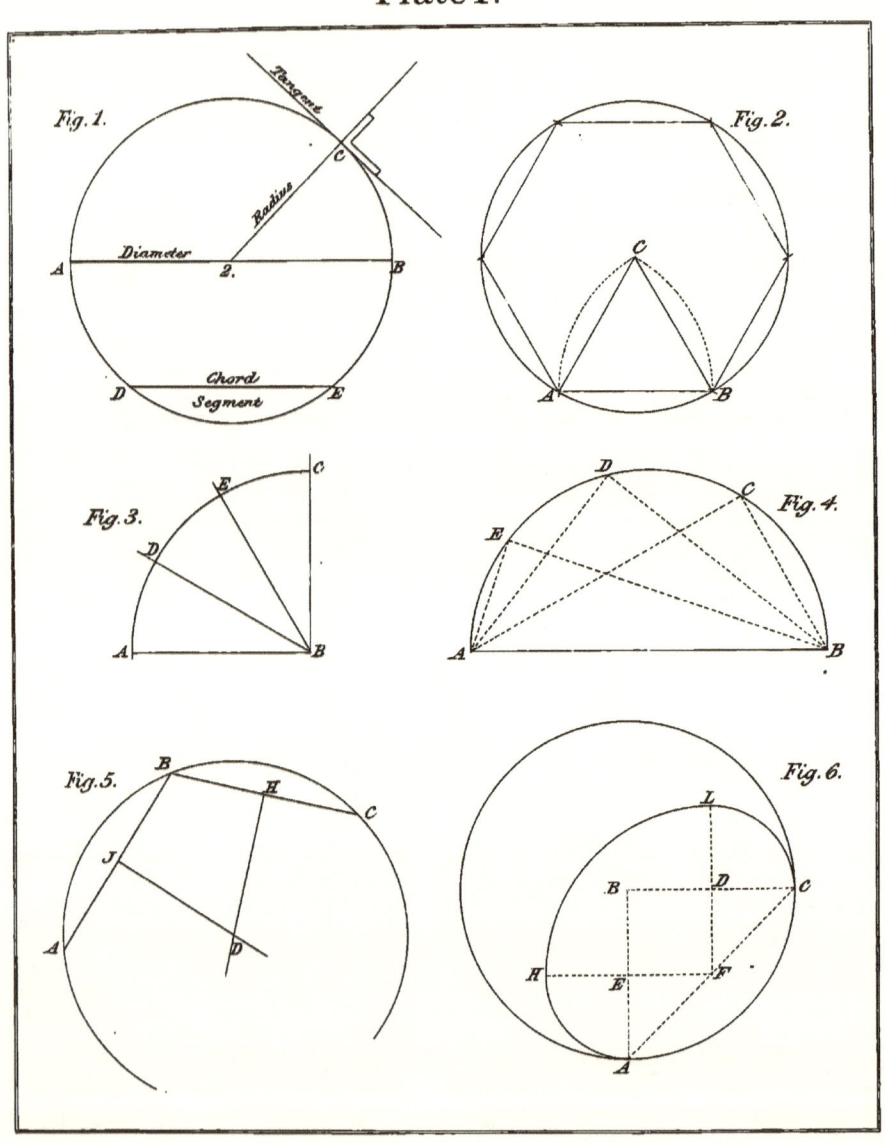

Plate 1.

MECHANICS, GEOMETRY.

THE illustrations on this and the following plates will show that the whole principle of practical geometry consists of but three representations—namely, the Circle, Square, and Triangle. These combine with other geometrical figures in endless variety, and are all constantly employed in almost every mechanical art.

Fig. 1 shows a circle, said to be a plain figure bounded by a curved line, all parts of which are equally distant from one point, called the centre. The diameter is a line passing through the centre, and cutting the circumference, as A B. The radius of a circle is a line drawn from the centre to circumference, as 2 C. The tangent means a line touching the circle, as at C, square with it and 2. The chord is a line which cuts off a portion of a circle, and terminates in the circumference both ways, as D E.

The above definitions should be remembered, in order that the explanations of other figures may be understood by the learner.

Fig. 2. Here is a circle, the radius of which divides its circumference into six equal parts, and lines being drawn to each part it forms a hexagon, or figure of six sides, and on one of which, as A B, may be constructed the equilateral triangle. This means a figure of three equal sides; it is drawn by taking A B as radius, also centres; describe the arcs, cutting each other at C; join it with A B, and we have an equilateral triangle; observe that its sides are parallel with those of the hexagon.

Fig. 3. To trisect a right angle or quadrant into three equal parts, take A as centre, and B radius; intersect the quadrant at E; take C as centre, and with same radius intersect at D; thus the quadrant is divided into three equal parts.

Fig. 4 shows a semicircle; all the angles inscribed in it are right angles. For example, draw from A, cutting any point, say C, join it and B; thus a right angle is formed.

Again, draw from A, say to D; join it and B; the result is the same. Or take A E B; the angle is still the same.

This valuable problem will be often brought into requisition in the illustration of practical works which are yet to come.

Fig. 5. Any three points not in a straight line must be in a circle; or, to put the question in another form, any three fingers of the hand are in a circle; you cannot make them touch a straight line without bending. This problem is of value and importance, as will be shown a little farther on; but, to solve it, place the thumb on A, and next finger say on B, and third finger on C; join these letters, and bisect A B at J; draw from it square with A B; now bisect B C at H; draw from it square with B C, cutting at D, which is a centre for describing a circle that will pass through A B C.

Fig. 6. To inscribe an oval in a circle; draw from centre B, the right angle A B C; divide A C at F, draw from it parallel with A B, and B C, cutting at E and D, which are centres, to draw quadrants A H and C L; then F is also a centre to draw quadrant H L, and the figure is complete.

PLATE 2.

THE MEASUREMENT OF SURFACES BY GEOMETRICAL CONSTRUCTION.

FIGURE 1 shows a rectangle, as A B C D. Extend A D and C B; divide A B at H, and D C at F; draw from D through H, cutting at J; draw from B through F, cutting at E; this gives a figure as J B E D, and its surface is just equal to that of the rectangle A B C D. This fact is self-evident, because, if we cut off angle J B H, it will fit that of B C F; and in like manner the angle E D F being cut off, it must fit that of D A H; thus proving the surfaces of both figures to be equal.

Fig. 2. To construct two unequal squares so that the surface of the larger shall measure double that of the smaller. For example, let A B C D be any square. Draw from B through D, and from C through A; make L H and L K equal B D; complete the other two sides of the square; then the surface of L H N K is double that of A B C D.

The solution of this problem is the answer to a question that is often put.

Thus: Here is a rod one inch square (its length immaterial). Now we wish you to produce another rod exactly one-half, or double the square of the first; or we may take a pocket-handkerchief twenty-four inches square, and wish it reduced to one-half its original size, or another just double its size. Figure 2 shows the rule to do this.

Fig. 3. The circle D and semicircle A B C have equal surfaces.

The construction is as follows: Draw line B C; divide it at 2; make C D equal C 2; then D is a centre from which describe a circle; its surface will be found equal to that of the semicircle A B C.

Fig. 4. To describe two circles of unequal diameters, the surface of the smaller to measure half that of the larger. Take any point, as A, on diameter, and with any radius, as D, draw a circle cutting diameter at L, square up from it, and make L N equal L A; join N A. This line having cut at D gives a point from which draw parallel with N L, cutting at C as centre and D radius for small circle; its surface will be found one-half that of large circle.

This problem is sometimes used for proportions of columns or cylinders; this means that it will give the proportion of half or double in diameters.

Fig. 5. To find a straight line that shall equal the circumference of a circle or quadrant. For example, take the semicircle A B C; draw the chord B C; divide it at P; join it and A; then four times P A are equal to the circumference of a circle whose diameter is A C, or equal to curve C B.

To divide the quadrant A B into any number of equal parts, say thirteen. To do this, lay the rule on, and make A R measure 3¼ inches, which are thirteen quarters or parts on the rule; make R 2 equal one-quarter inch; join R P; draw from 2 parallel with R P, cutting at V; now take P V in the dividers, and set off from A on the circle thirteen parts, which end at B; each part being equal to P V, and we have the solution.

Fig. 6. To construct two equal angles on any two given lines, as A B and D B. Draw from A any angle, as A C; take A as centre, and with any radius draw the arc, say B C; come to D, take it as centre, and with same radius draw the arc B E; make it measure equal to that of B C; then draw from D through E, and we have two equal angles.

This is a simple problem, yet it will be often brought into requisition as an assistant for many of our most important constructions.

Plate 2.

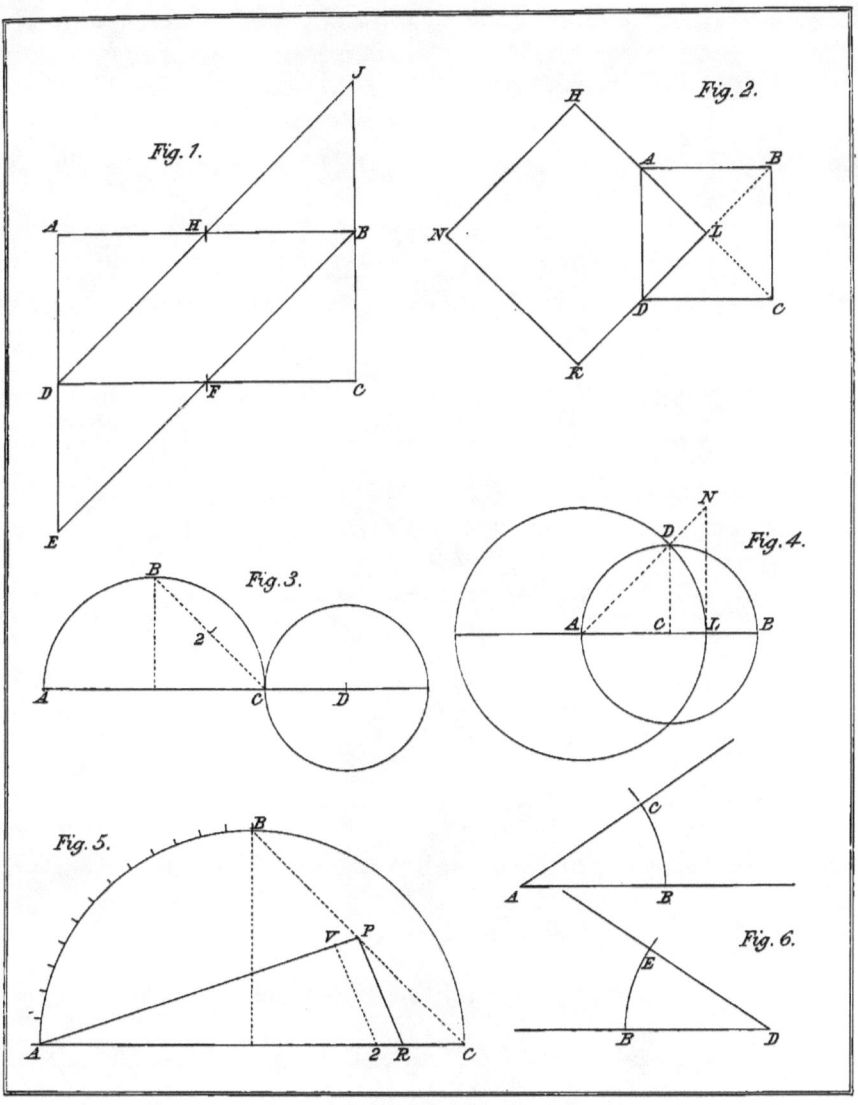

Plate 3.

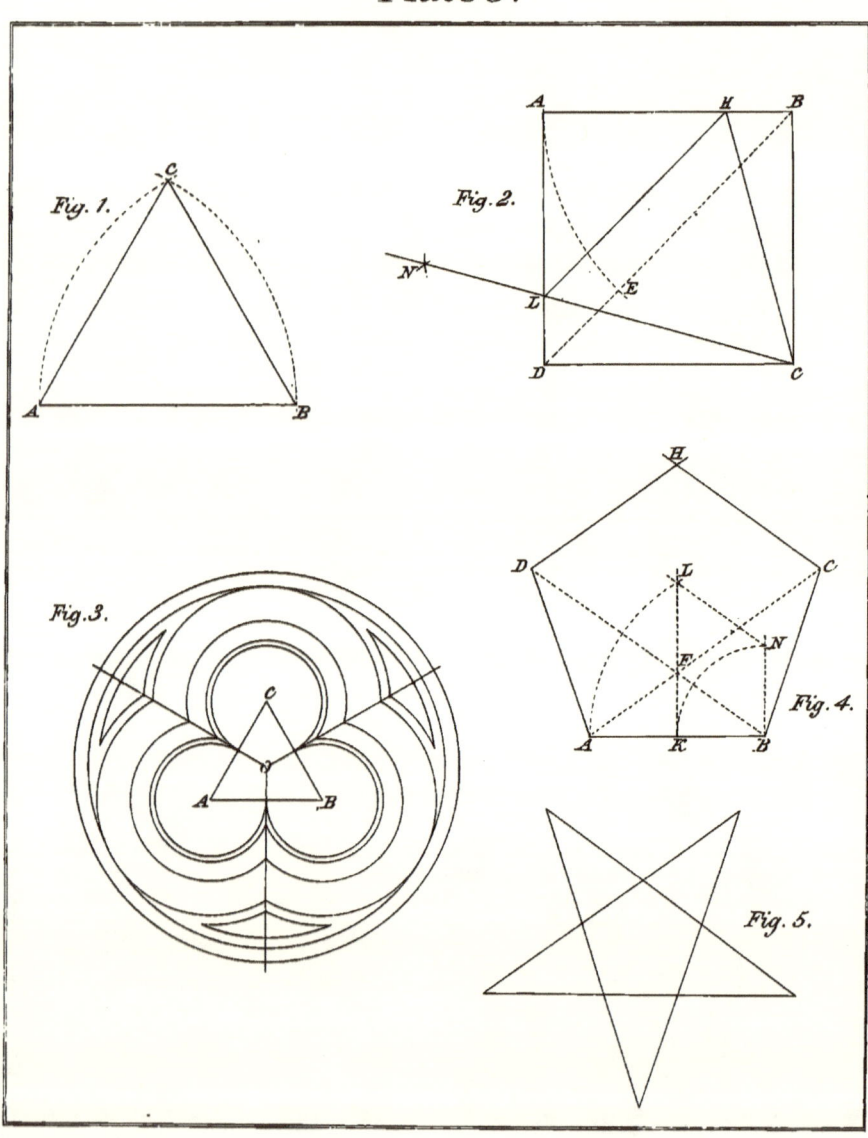

Fig. 1.

Fig. 2.

Fig. 3.

Fig. 4.

Fig. 5.

PLATE 3.

FIGURE 1. To construct the equilateral triangle on a given line, as A B, which take for radius, also centres. Describe circles cutting each other at C; join C with A and B, thus producing a figure of three equal sides.

Fig. 2. To construct the largest equilateral triangle that a given square will contain. Draw the diagonal B D; take D as centre, and A radius; draw the circle cutting at E; take it as centre, and A radius; describe an arc at N, with same radius, and A centre; intersect the arc at N, from which point draw to C; make B H equal D L; join H C L, and the problem is solved.

Fig. 3. Here is shown one of the uses to which the equilateral triangle may be put in describing a figure called the *trefoil*, which is often introduced in the construction of windows and other ornamental work. Each corner of the triangle, as A B C, is a centre from which are struck all the inner curves, and the outer circles being struck from centre, O. The construction is so simple and self-evident as not to require further explanation.

Fig. 4. To construct a pentagon on a given line, as A B, which divide at K, square up from it and B; take B as centre, and A radius; draw the circle cutting at L, with same centre, and K radius; draw circle cutting at N; join it and L; draw from B parallel with N L; this having cut at F gives a point through which draw from A; make F C D equal A B; join C B and D A; draw from C parallel with B D; draw from D parallel with A C, cutting at H, *which completes the pentagon by parallels.*

Fig. 5 shows a pentagon. Its sides, being extended, produce a figure that may be used in ornamental works.

PLATE 4.

FIGURE 1. To construct a hexagon on a given line, as A B, which take for radius, also centres; describe the circles, cutting each other at C; draw from A and B, through C; draw from B, parallel with A C, and from A parallel with B C; make B F and A H equal A B, also make C D and C E equal A B; join F D E H, which completes the hexagon, a figure of six equal sides.

Here it may be mentioned that the greatest pains should be taken in having all drawings correct, and especially those for practical purposes. The following figure will show clearly the necessity for it.

Fig. 2 shows a portion of a pavement in wood, stone, or other material. Here it is clear that if the least error is made, either in drawing or working even one of the triangles, that error alone would make it impossible to form the hexagon, and naturally spoil the work, which shows to the workman the necessity of attention and correctness in his drawing as well as in his work.

Fig. 3. To construct a figure of seven equal sides on a given line, as A B, which divide at K, square up from it; now take A B for radius and B centre; intersect line from K at L; with same radius and A centre, draw the circle 2 3; now take K L as radius, and from 2, as centre, intersect the circle at 3; draw from it to B, cutting at N, through which point draw from A; make A D equal B 3; join A 3

and B D; draw from 3, parallel with A D; draw from B through L, cutting at C; join it and A; draw from 3 parallel with A C; make 3 H equal A B, and C E equal N D; join E D; draw from H parallel with 3 C, cutting at F; join it and E, which completes the heptagon. This figure is but seldom required in practice, yet here it serves as an exercise, and illustrates a principle of drawing by parallels.

Fig. 4 shows a method of forming the model of a pyramid; it having six equal sides standing on a hexagon base; the drawing being on card-board. Let one side of the pyramid, as A B, work on a hinge by making a slight cut on line A B, and in like manner cut the sides in order that they may fold against the base and form the pyramid which terminates in point C. It will, however, be best to cut off the sides below C, as shown.

This illustration for a model is merely intended as an introduction to card-board, which may be cut and made to show either accuracy or defects in any construction before any attempt is made on actual work.

The best tool for cutting card-board is a piece of well-tempered steel, about six or seven inches long, ⅜ of an inch wide, and ⅛ thick, ground from both sides to a point similar to letter V; or take a small chisel and grind it to the form stated. A tool of this description will be found much better than a knife.

12

Plate 4.

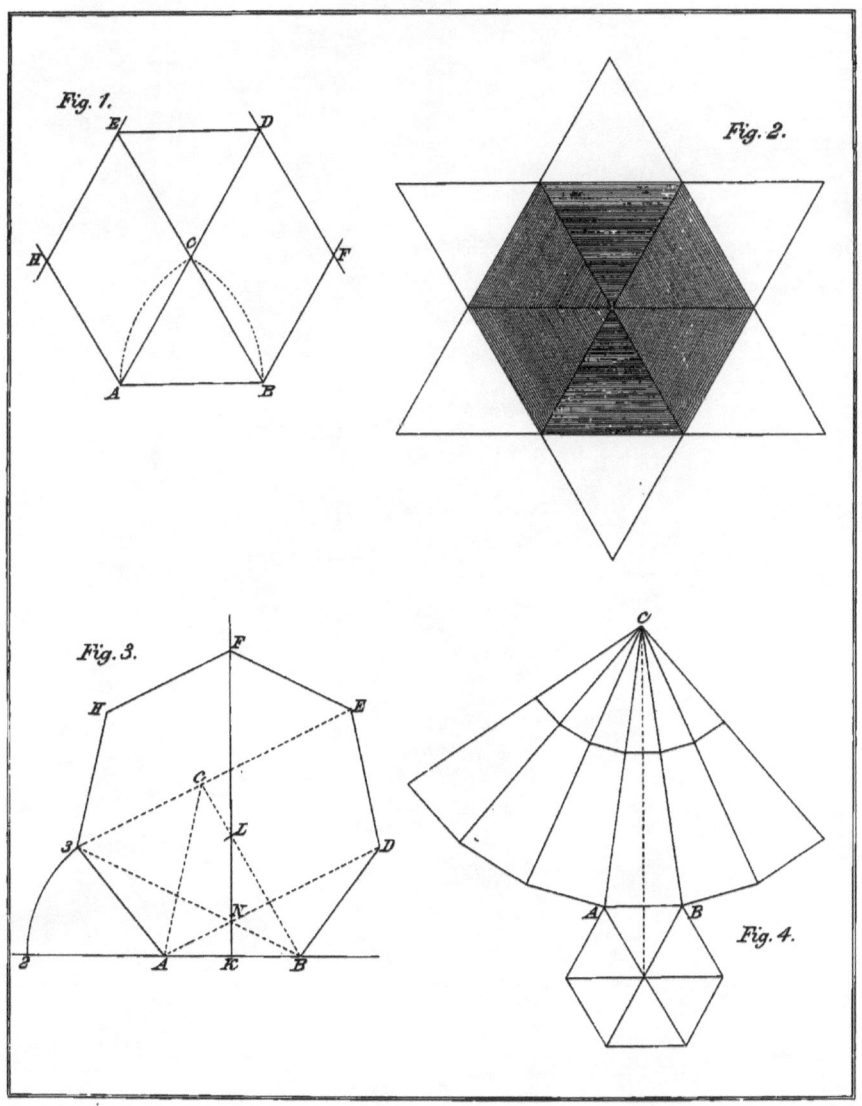

Fig. 1.

Fig. 2.

Fig. 3.

Fig. 4.

Plate 5.

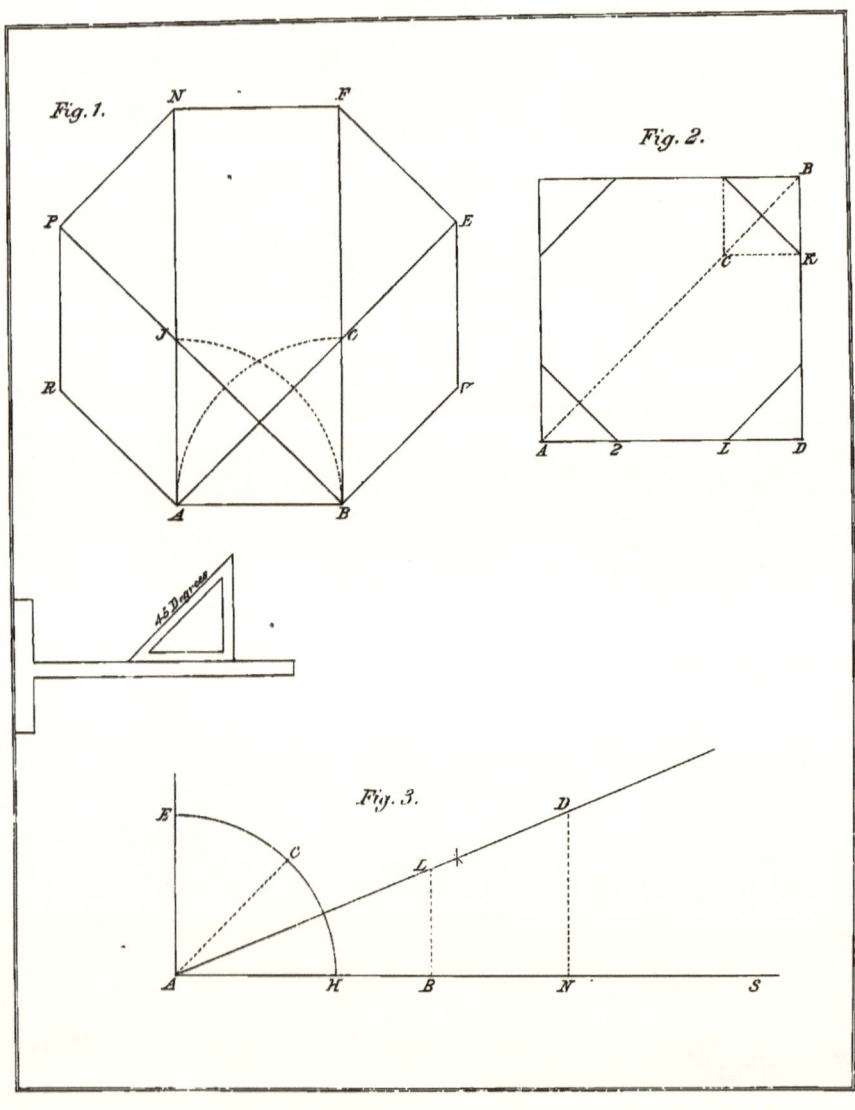

Fig. 1.

Fig. 2.

Fig. 3.

45 Degree

PLATE 5.

THE OCTAGON.

FIGURE 1. To construct an octagon, one of its sides being given as A B, from which square up two lines. Take A B as radius, also centres; draw the circles cutting at C and J; draw from A B through C J; again from A draw parallel with B J; draw from B parallel with A C; make B V and C E equal A B; join E V; make C F equal C A; square over F N; join F E; draw N P parallel with A C; join P R.

This completes a figure of eight equal sides, or octagon. The same may be quickly done by using both a T and set-square, the latter having an angle of 45° as shown.

Fig. 2. To work the octagon in a practical way. This means that if a piece of square timber is given, and it is required to work it to eight equal sides, proceed by drawing a line from corner to corner, as A B; make A C equal one side of the square, as A D; square over C K; set a gauge to B K; run this on sides of stuff; work off the corners, and we have *eight equal sides.*

Fig. 3. To construct a scale by which the side of any octagon is known at once.

Commence and make any right angle, as that from A; take it as centre, and with any radius draw the quadrant E H; divide it at C; take C as centre, and with any radius make an arc at L; with same radius and centre H intersect the arc, through which draw from A, and the scale is complete. To prove it, make A N equal A N, Fig. 1; square up from N, cutting at D; then N D is found equal to A B, Fig. 1. As a further proof, make A B equal A D, Fig. 2; square up from B, cutting at L; then B L equals 2 L, Fig. 2.

This simple method gives the side of any octagon without drawing the whole figure.

PLATE 6.

FIGURE 1. To find a straight line that shall equal a quadrant or semicircle. Take A B radius, and A centre; intersect the circle at C; join it and B; draw from D, parallel with C B, cutting at H; then A H will be found equal to curve A D.

This method is somewhat different to that already given; both, however, are practical.

Fig. 2. To find a straight line which is equal to the circumference of a circle. Draw from centre, O, any right angle, cutting at J and V; join J V; draw from O parallel with J V; square down from J, cutting at N; join it and V; then four times N V will be found to equal the circumference.

I am not aware that this and the previous simple methods have ever before been given in any publication.

Plate 6.

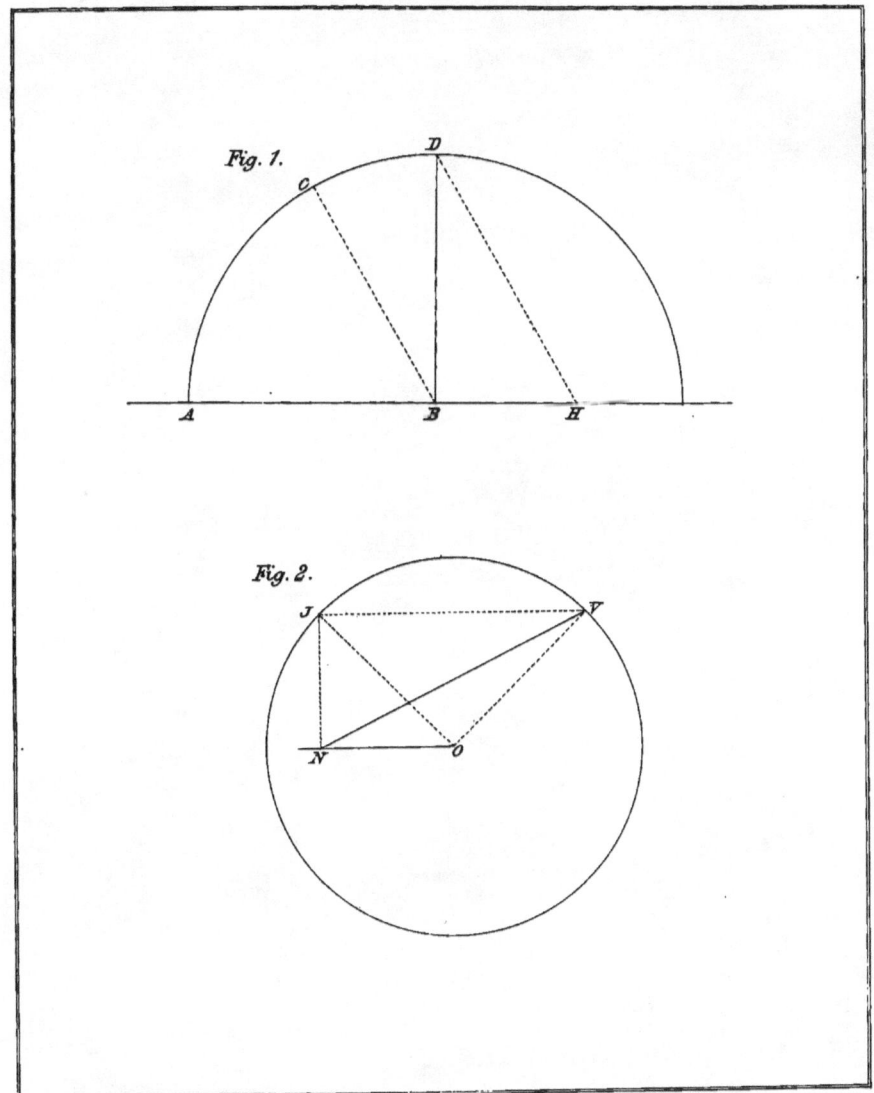

Fig. 1.

Fig. 2.

Plate 7.

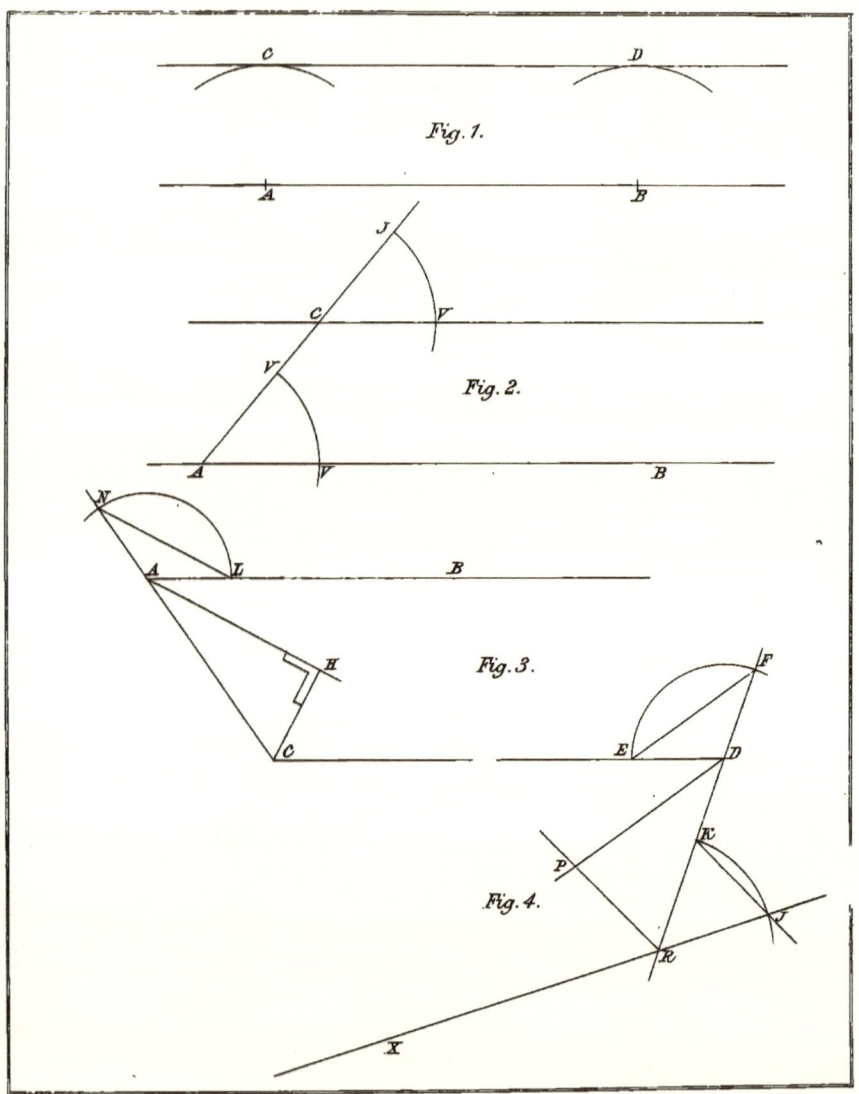

c   D

Fig. 1.

A   B

Fig. 2.

Fig. 3.

Fig. 4.

PLATE 7.

TO DRAW PARALLEL LINES; AND BISECT IRREGULAR ANGLES.

FIGURE 1. To draw a line parallel with a given line, as A B. Take A for centre and C radius; draw an arc through point C, then, with same radius, take any point on given line as B; draw the arc D; now draw through C D, and the line is parallel with that of A B.

Fig. 2. SECOND METHOD. — Assume A B as the given line, and C a point through which a parallel is to pass; draw through C, at any angle, cutting A; take it as centre, and, with any radius, draw arc V V; with same radius, and C centre, draw arc J V; make it measure equal to that of V V; then a line drawn through C V is parallel to that of A B.

Fig. 3. To bisect acute or obtuse angles, extend line C A; take A as centre, and with any radius draw an arc, cutting at N L, which join; draw from A, parallel with N L; draw from C; square with line from A, cutting at H, and angles A C are bisected.

Fig. 4. To bisect acute or obtuse angles when two of the sides are not parallel, as is the case here. For example, the lines D E and R X are sides; then extend the end R D, and side X R; take D as centre, and with any radius draw the circle, cutting at E F, which join; draw from D, parallel with F E; this done, come to R, take it as centre, and with any radius draw the circle, cutting at K J, which join; draw from R, parallel with K J, intersecting line from D at P: thus the angles are bisected.

This will be found a valuable and useful problem in laying out framing, mitring mouldings, finding the seats of hip-rafters, and it may also be applied to many other practical purposes.

PLATE 8.

TO FIND CURVES OF ANY SPAN AND RISE WITHOUT USING A CENTRE.

FIGURE 1. To construct an arch of any span and of any rise without using a centre. For example, assume A B as the span and O O as rise. Now take a piece of board, as that of Fig. 2; draw on it a semicircle; make its radius O O equal rise of arch; set off from each side of O on circle any number of equal parts, say four; and in like manner set off four parts on each side of O, at base; join the parts on base and circle by lines, as 1 1, 2 2, 3 3; these lines are drawn to cut upper edge of board, as shown.

Now come to span or chord A B, and set off on right and left of O four parts; bring upper edge of board, Fig. 2, against the chord A B; make line 1, 1 through semicircle come opposite point 1 on chord A B; extend the line by a straight edge, and make distance 1, 1 equal to 1, 1 on semicircle; move the board until line 2 2 comes opposite point 2 on chord; draw line 2 2 in the same direction as that of 2 2 through semicircle; make the distance of both equal; slide the board along the chord in this manner, and mark lines from the chord in the same direction as those through semicircle; then corresponding letters and distances of both being the same gives points into which drive nails as a guide to bend a strip; mark the curve by it, and the work is complete.

This method will be found more simple and more reliable for large or small curves than any other that has yet been devised.

Fig. 3. To construct a flat curve or arch, its span, say sixteen feet and its rise only two inches. Take, for example, the camber on a joist or beam. To do this by a practical and ready method, have a board of sufficient length and parallel width, joint one edge; divide the length into two parts, as line L; divide the joist in like manner, and from the top edge of it, at the extreme ends, set off two inches, as A B; drive a nail into each; lay the board on, and bring its jointed edge against the nails; then force lower edge until its upper edge L reaches point N. Now mark the curve A N B, which is the camber required.

Here it is understood that the method just given is for a pattern by which a flat curve may be marked on joist or anything else; the span, of course, being limited to length of board, which bends and forms the curve.

Plate 8.

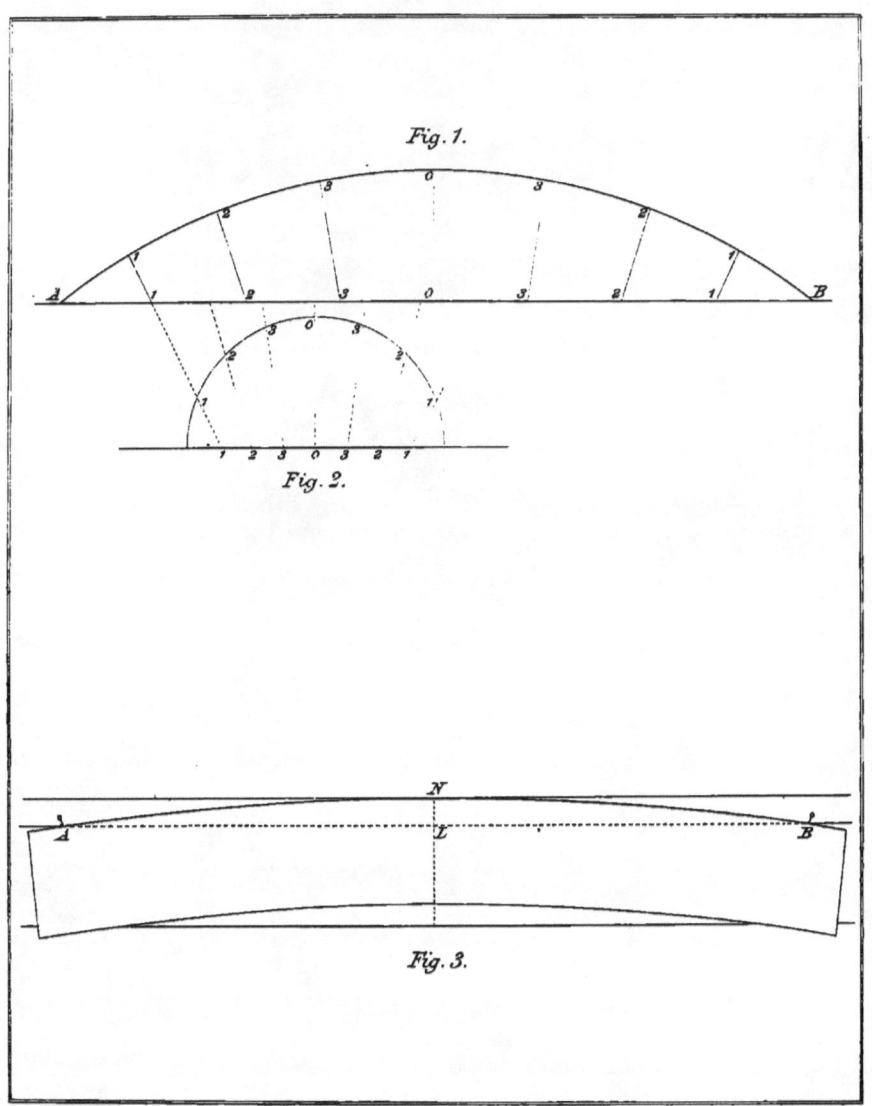

Fig. 1.

Fig. 2.

Fig. 3.

Plate 9.

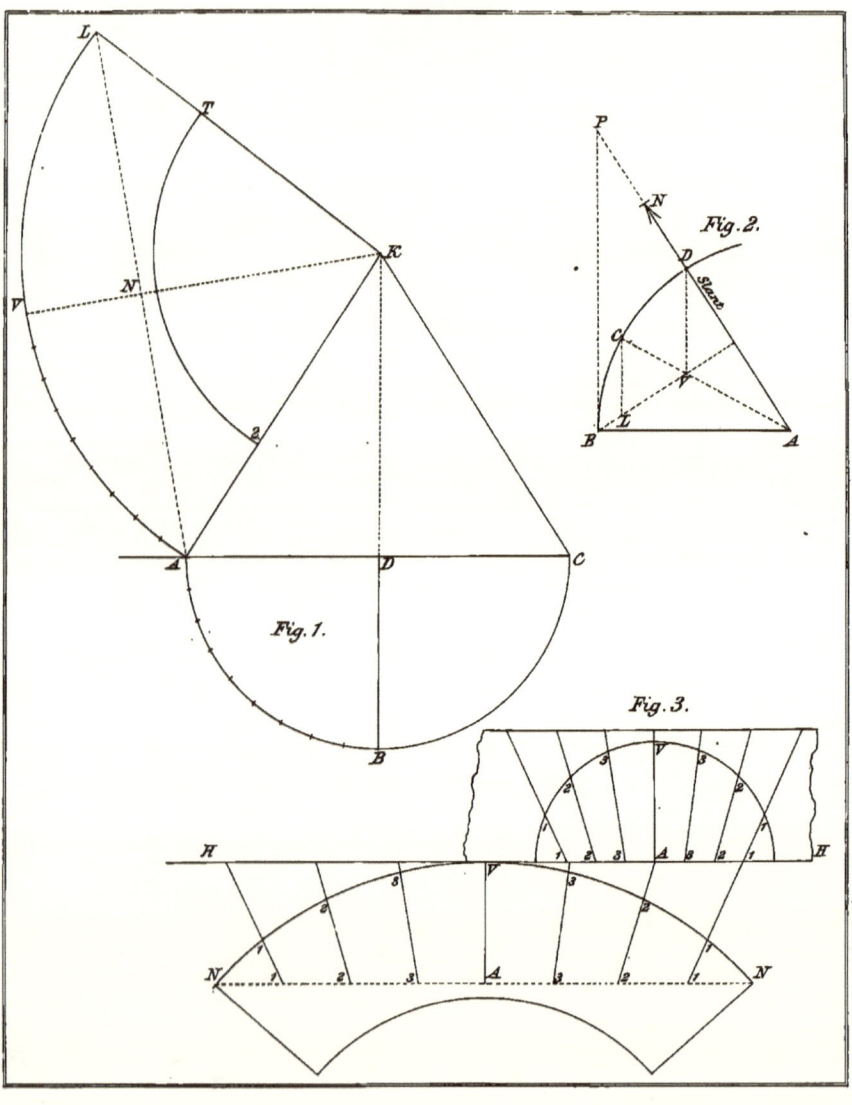

Fig.1.

Fig.2.

Fig.3.

PLATE 9.

THE CONE.

FIGURE 1. Shows the base of half a cone, its sides terminating in point K. Perhaps there is nothing that a workman should be more thoroughly conversant with than that of covering a cone. It is of the greatest service to joiners, masons, metal plate-workers, and, in fact, every one connected with building trades. But, to give some idea of its value, suppose we are required to bend a piece of metal, board, or any other material to a curve, and it to stand on a given slant. For example, take the back of a pew, or even a tin dish with slanting sides, and scores of other things; all have a simple construction, that must be understood before any attempt can be made to give the material the desired shape. But, to explain this point, let us show the method by which the covering of a cone is obtained.

Take K as centre, and A radius; draw the circle A V L; divide the quadrant A B into say nine, or any number of equal parts; set off the same from A to V; make V L equal V A; take any width for covering, say A 2; draw the curve 2 T. This completes the work; and it is certainly simple, considering what has been said of its importance. But let us examine the matter a little further by cutting a piece of cardboard in the shape given for covering, then bend its edge A V L around the base A B C. Here notice that the lower edge, although curved, yet comes to a perfect level, and the face of the card-board stands on slant A K. This could not be done without some rule, and *that* just given is the one usually adopted, and a correct one.

But it sometimes happens that the work having a conical form and of large dimensions where it would be not only inconvenient but almost impracticable to find a centre for striking curves on lower and upper edges of the work; in such cases other means than those given must be used. The following new and simple problem obviates all difficulties.

Fig. 2. Let A B be the radius for base of work; or have it equal A D on the left, draw slant A D, extended, the slant having cut the circle at D, from which draw square with A B; draw from B square with slant cutting line from D at V; draw from A through V, cutting circle at C; square down from it, cutting line from B at L; make D N equal C L. This gives A N for half the chord, and is proved to be correct because it equals that of A N on the left; again D V is the rise; this is also proved correct by it being equal to N V on the left.

Here it is noticed that radius and slant at both places are alike, and purposely made so in order that this new problem may be tested.

The distance A P is radius; but it is not required, as we are assuming the work to be on an extensive scale where no centre can be used.

Fig. 3 shows the practical application of this new method. Let H H be the edge of a board which is to be curved in order to fit a circular base of a dome, cone, or slanting back for a circular pew. In either case, when the board is bent, its edges are to be level.

To find the curve. Have a piece of board as shown, and draw on it a semicircle, with radius A V, which corresponds with D V, Fig. 2; divide the circle on each side of V into any number of parts, say four, and in like manner set off on each side of A four equal parts; join the parts on circle and base by drawing lines, as 1 1, 2 2, 3 3. Now set off rise V A on the board which is to be bent; draw through A parallel with H H; make A N on right and left equal A N, Fig. 2; divide A N on right and left into four equal parts, as 1 1, 2 2, 3 3; now slide the board with semicircle along the edge H H, and at the same time make line 1 1; cut point 1 on chord N N; continue in this manner until the lines on face of board are drawn, and in the same direction as those on semicircle; make distance 1 1, 2 2, 3 3, on right and left equal corresponding distances and figures of semicircle; thus points are given to drive nails, against which bend a strip and mark the curve; the edge being worked, draw the width parallel with worked edge; both edges fall to a level when the board is bent, and stand on slant A D, Fig. 2.

Plate 10.

FIGURE 1. To construct a semi-ellipse by means of a string and two pins..

Nearly every one knows this problem. It is indispensable to the joiner, stair-builder, mason, metalworker, and even the gardener. The operation is simple. All that is requisite being at hand, namely, two pins, a linen thread or fine cord. The method is as follows: Assume A B as long diameter; divide it at 2; from which point square up a line, as 2 E; call this short diameter; take A 2 as radius; with same radius and E centre intersect long diameter at C and D; these are points into which fix two pins; tie a string to pin D; bring it around pin C; place the finger on string; stretch it with a pencil, making its point touch E; now sweep the curve to B; return to E, and complete the curve to A. This operation is done best by having a notch in the pencil near its point in order to keep the string from slipping.

Fig. 2 shows a method for describing a semi-ellipse by means of a rod. The two diameters, as A B and 2 L, being given, take a rod and mark on it the distance V N, which is equal to half of long diameter A 2; make V T equal short diameter 2 L; lay the rod on; keep mark T on line A B, and mark N on short diameter; move the rod a short distance, keeping T and N on diameters; mark a point at the end

of rod V; continue in this manner marking any number of points, through which trace a curve by bending a strip, and we have a semi-ellipse. This method answers to check any defect in the elliptic curve when drawn by a string, which might happen if the operation is done in a careless manner. Some adopt the method of having two brad-awls through the rod at marks T and N; the awls work against a fence which is fastened on the two diameters. Both these methods are tedious and not equal to the string, which is quick, practical, and off-hand.

Fig. 3. To find tangents on any part of an elliptic curve. Let A B be the long diameter and 2 N the short; take A 2 as radius; with same radius and N centre intersect long diameter at C and D. Now find a tangent at any point, say L; join it and C; draw from D parallel with L C; take D as centre and L as radius; draw the circle cutting at P; draw from it through L, and we have a tangent. Assume any other point, say J; join it and D; draw from C parallel with J D; take C as centre and J as radius; draw the circle cutting at T; draw from it through J, and a tangent is the result. It is understood that long and short diameters must be at right angles for every ellipse; therefore a tangent, as that through N, it, and the short diameter, must always be at right angles, as shown.

30

Plate 10.

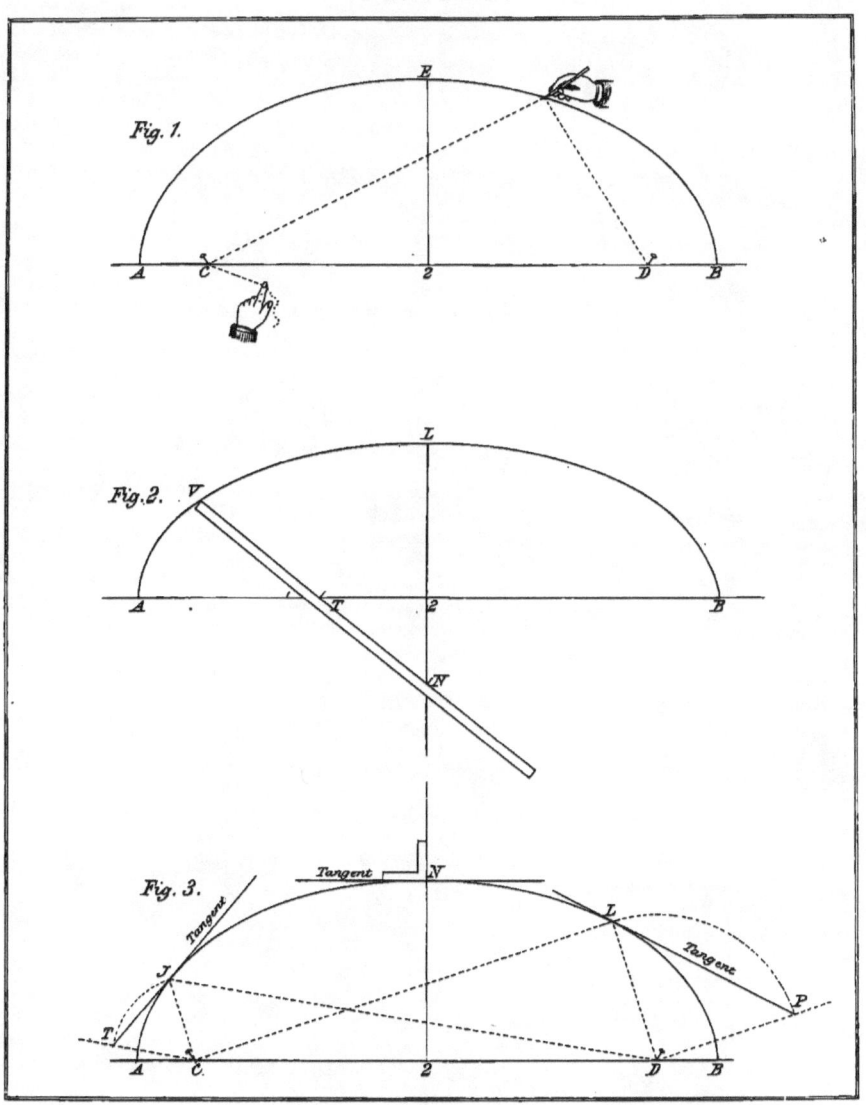

Fig. 1.

Fig. 2.

Fig. 3.

Tangent

Plate 11.

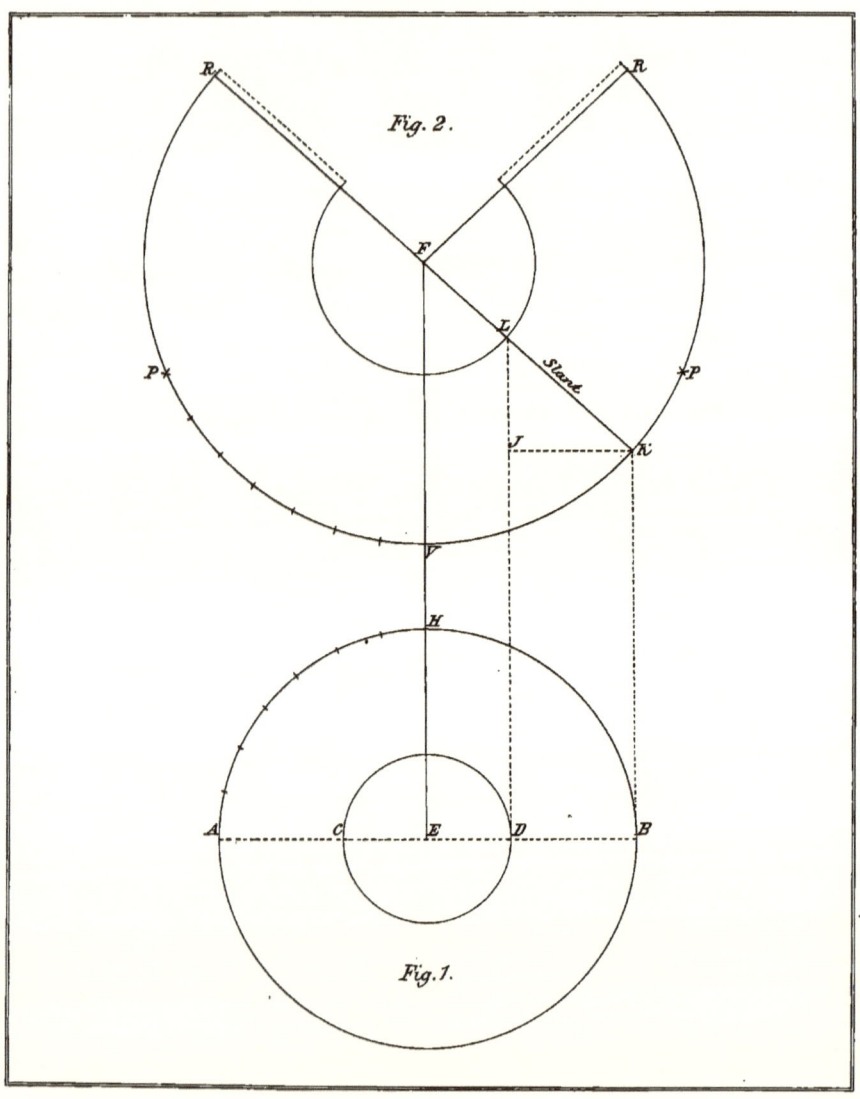

Fig. 2.

Fig. 1.

PLATE 11.

TO CONSTRUCT SLANTING WORK STANDING ON A CIRCULAR BASE.

THIS plate shows a practical construction by which the joiner is directed in finding the form of boards or framing that stand on a slant around a circular base.

Fig. 1 shows the problem by which the metal-plate worker cuts and shapes his material in forming a can, a circular flange, a tapering pipe, or anything having the form of a cone, — even the sailor uses it, or something similar, in finding the shape of a piece of canvas that will slant from the deck and inclose the mast as a protection against leakage. Many other purposes might be named to which this valuable problem applies. To illustrate it, let us consider the large circle as the base of a cone, its upper part cut off, making the small circle C D. We now want to find a covering that will go around the large circle and stand on a given slant. To do this, draw diameter A B. Square up from E D B. Take any point, as K, square over from it to J. Return to K, and draw from it the slant which the work is to have, say that of K L. This line, having cut the perpendiculars from the base at L F, gives L K as width of covering and J L as perpendicular height

of work, and F as centre to strike the curves through L K, which being done, divide the quadrant A H at Fig. 1 into any number of parts, as seven ; set off the same from V to P on left of Fig. 2 ; make P R equal P V ; set off V P R on the right to equal corresponding letters and distances on the left ; draw through R R on right and left, and the covering is complete. If the work is to be in metal, then allow for a lap, as indicated by dotted lines.

To have a practical illustration of this problem, take a piece of stiff paper and cut it to the shape of covering ; this being done, bring the joints R R together, which contracts the circles and makes their diameters just equal to those of A B and C D at the base of Fig. 1. We also see that the side stands exactly on the given slant K L.

This practical method shows how easy and simple the means are by which we can accomplish some of the most difficult kinds of work in either wood, metal, or stone. Understand that this problem is not limited to the few useful purposes just named, but it is equally applicable to many other branches of art.

PLATE 12.

THE PYRAMID IN CARD-BOARD.

To construct a pyramid, which means a figure with a square base and slanting sides.

This and similar forms frequently occur in the practice of joiners, masons, and metal plate-workers.

Fig. 1 shows the base; erect on one of its sides the triangle A B V; draw from A and B through V; draw from it parallel with A B; make V F and V S, also V H, equal A B; join A F S H; the four sides of pyramid are now spread out; these, when in position, inclose and terminate in point V, as may be clearly shown by having the drawing on card-board and cut; but before this is done, one or two other important points should be known, namely, the slant and perpendicular height of sides; these are found by squaring up from B and drawing V L square with A B; take L as centre and V radius; draw the circle cutting at E; draw from it through L; then E L is slant of sides, and B E their perpendicular height. Now suppose the sides are to be mitred at each angle; this would require a bevel, which is found by making B C equal B L; take B as centre, and for radius a circle touching L E, cutting at D; join it and C, and you have the bevel, as shown.

It may, however, be that the sides are not to mitre. In that case the sides make butt-joints, and for which a bevel has to be found to apply on edges of work; L K, being square with slant.

It is obtained by taking any point, say R; square down from it, cutting at P; take R as centre, and for radius a circle touching L K, cutting at J; join it and P, thus giving the bevel shown to be applied on edges of sides.

This completes a very important construction, which may be more fully understood by cutting clear through three sides of a square base, and a slight cut on line A B, so as to form a hinge; this done, cut clear through B V H and all outer lines from H down to A; now make a slight cut on line V S and V F, also V A. These cuts form hinges; lift the piece and fold the sides on base, and the result is a model of a pyramid having its base square, its sides slanting, and terminate in a point. This and similar illustrations, by means of card-board, is of more practical value to workmen than a hundred drawings on a flat surface, which may not be understood by more than one out of ten.

Plate 12.

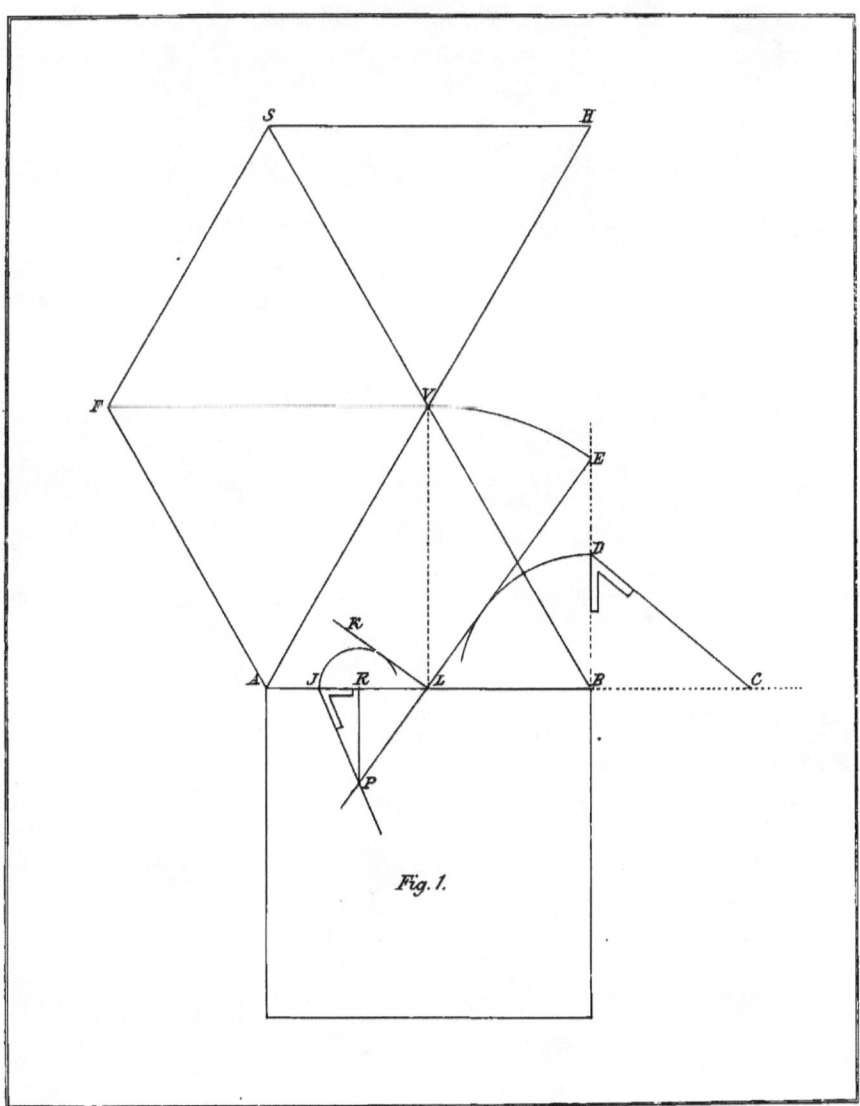

Fig. 1.

Plate 13.

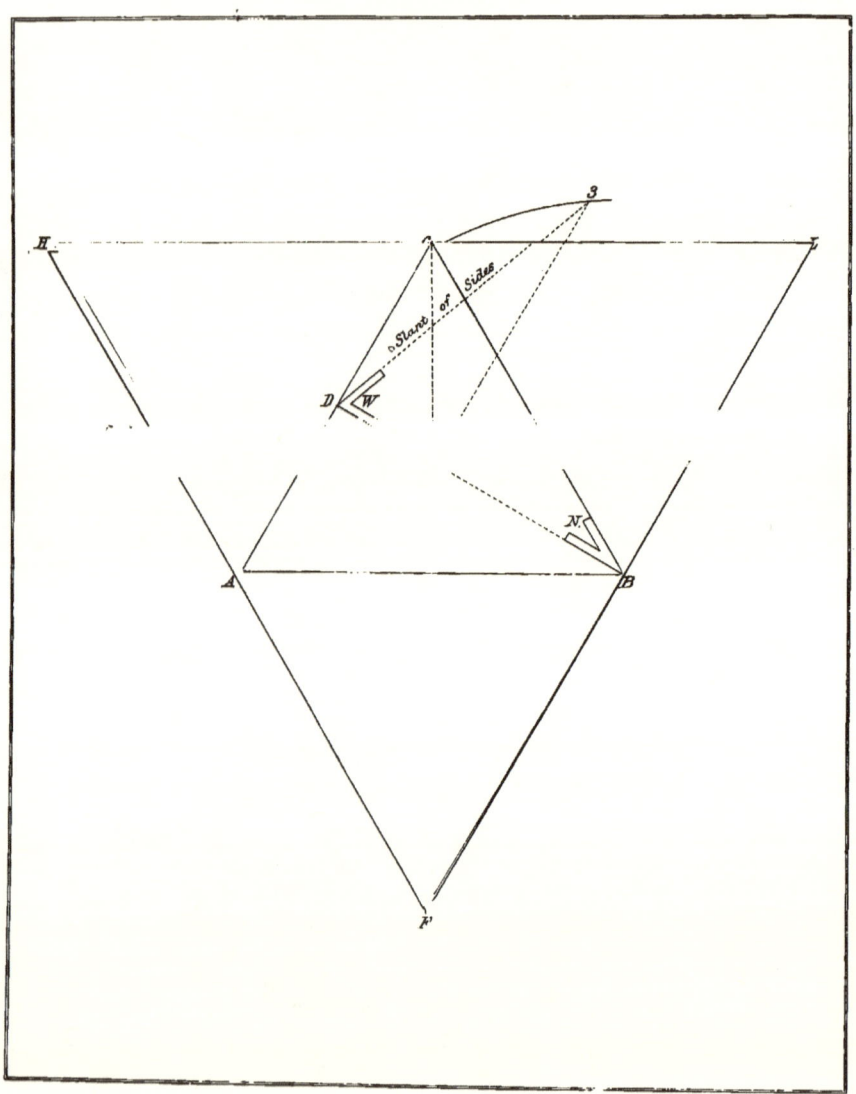

PLATE 13.

CONSTRUCTION OF A TRIANGULAR PYRAMID.

IN order that the actual construction of any piece of work may be fairly and clearly understood by young beginners or learners, we have cut a few models for this publication, which will show how simple the means are of forming them out of cardboard, and the great advantages to be derived from such practical illustrations.

The construction on this plate is simply a pyramid in the shape of an equilateral triangle. It will be observed that any of the triangles forms a base, as may be seen by lifting the piece and folding it from you. This to some might appear trifling, and of little moment; such, however, is not the case, as will be seen by laying the piece in its original position, that we may explain its construction.

Let A B C be the base. Draw through C parallel with A B; make C H and C L equal A B; draw from H L through A B, intersecting at F. Here we have four equal triangles, three of which form the sides of pyramid.

It is now required to show slant of sides and perpendicular height of work. To do this, draw from B, square with A C, cutting at D; draw from C, square with A B, cutting at 2; draw from it square with D B; take B as centre, and C as radius; draw the circle, cutting at 3; join it and D; this gives 3 D as slant of sides, and 2·8 for perpendicular height of pyramid.

Now suppose the sides are separate pieces of wood, stone, or metal, and these are to be mitred. To do this. Work the lower edge of base by bevel W; this being done, apply bevel N, and mark the mitre on edge which has been worked. Thus a direction is given to mitre the sides with the least possible trouble.

PLATE 14.

TO CONSTRUCT SLANTING SIDES TO STAND ON AN OCTAGON BASE.

THE material may be either wood or sheet-metal; if the latter, the sides and base may be in one piece.

The intention here is to have the drawing on card-board, and cut in such a manner as to form a perfect model of the work, by which means the learner sees the necessity of being correct in drawing every line; for, if the work is done properly on card-board, it is evident that the same practice applies to any other material, be it wood, stone, or metal.

The octagon base being given, we must now have a bevel for cut on face of slanting sides. It is found by drawing a line through any two angles of the base. For instance, draw from 2 through F; take any point on the line, say P; draw through it parallel with F L; now determine on slant of sides, say P K; take any point as C, square down from it, cutting at D; take it as centre, and C radius; draw the arc of circle, with same radius and P centre; draw arc A K; make it and arc C K equal; draw from K square with C D, cutting at S; square up from it, cutting at V; join it and D. This gives bevel W, to apply for cut on face of sides. Let us now find a bevel for mitre on edge of stuff. To do this, draw P T square with P K; take C as centre, and for radius a circle touching P T, cutting at J; draw from D through J; this gives bevel X for mitre on edge of stuff. The drawing being on card-board, and intended for a model, two of its sides, as H H, on right and left, are hinged to the base by making a slight cut on line H H. The bevel W being applied as shown, gives the cut on face of sides. Their position as spread out is found by drawing equal circles on each side as shown. The same, however, may be done by having a pattern, which is obtained by bevel W.

All that now remains is to cut clear through the outer and inner lines; this done, make a slight cut through each joint, in order to form a hinge. The cutting being done, lift the piece, fold the sides from you on the octagon base, and we have a correct model of the work.

Plate 14.

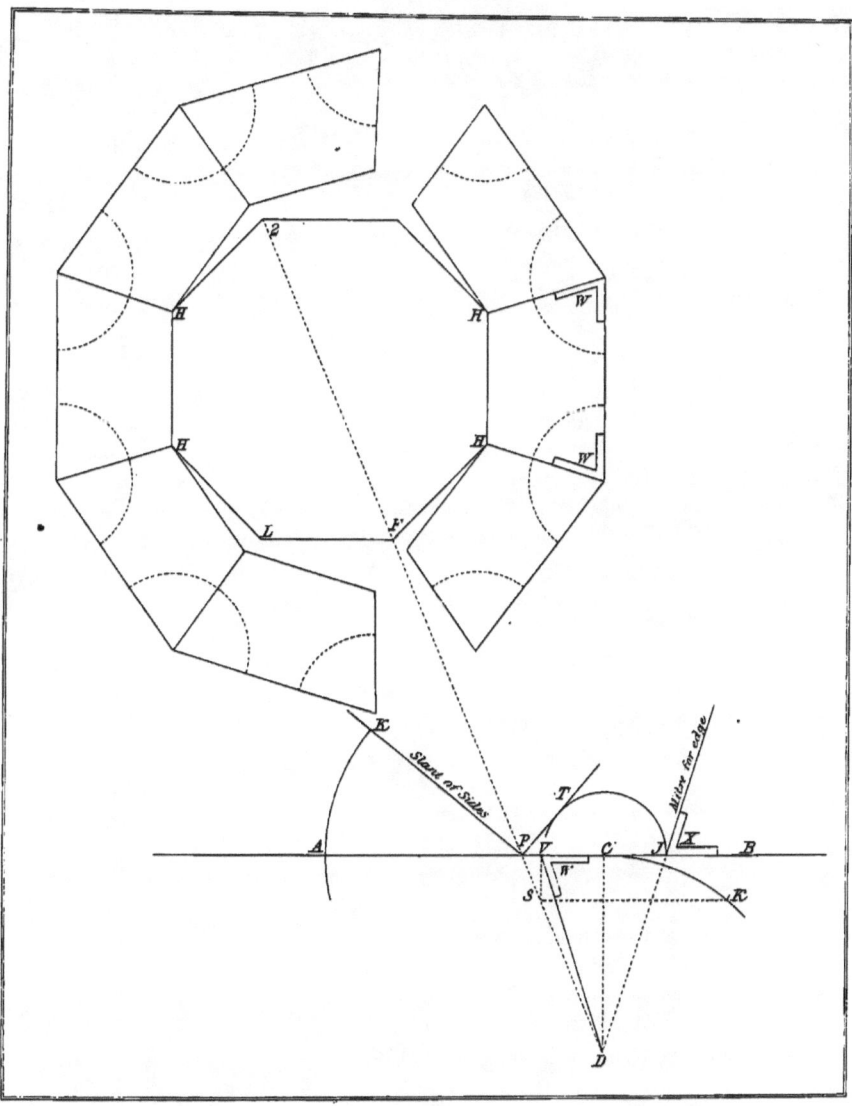

Plate 15.

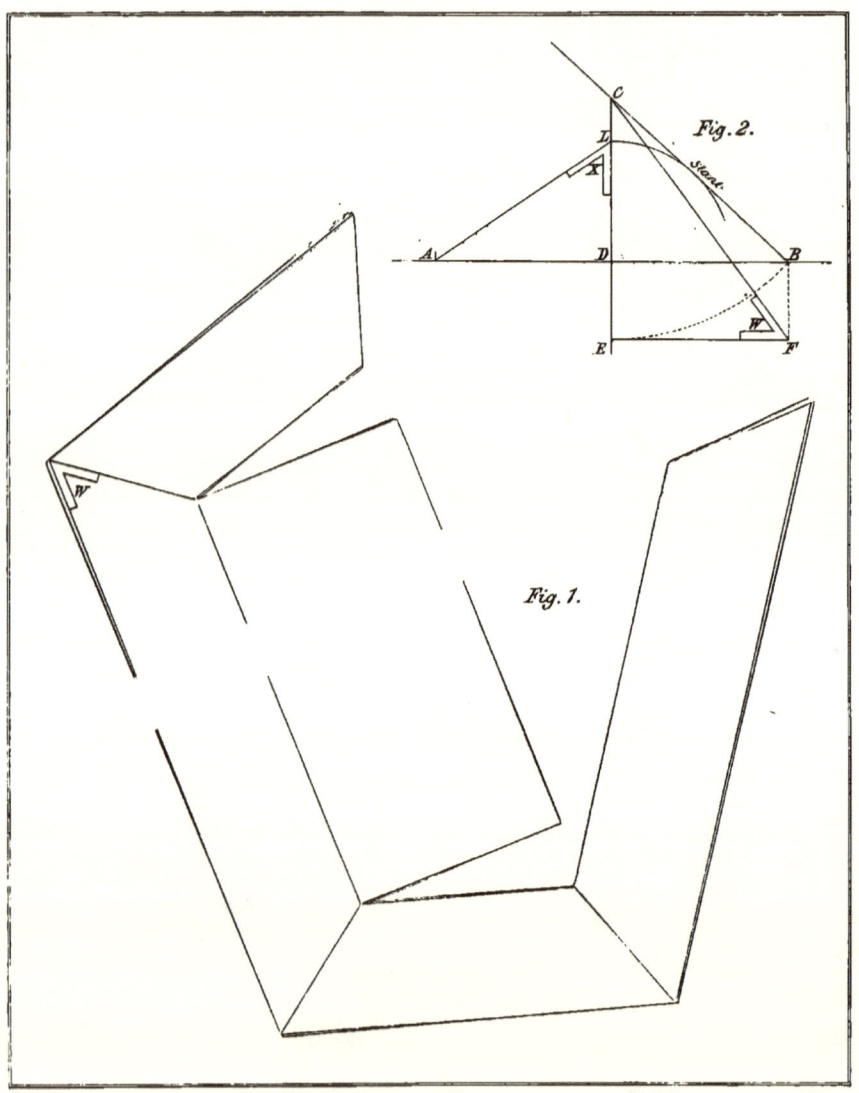

Fig. 2.

Fig. 1.

PLATE 15.

TO CONSTRUCT SLANTING SIDES TO A BASE HAVING RIGHT ANGLES.

FIGURE 1. The practical solution of this problem is before us. The card-board having been already cut to represent the actual work, lift the piece and fold the sides from you. Here we have a perfect model. Examine it thoroughly, and think for a moment if this practical illustration could be given by mere cutting and guessing, and without rule or guidance. Certainly not!

Then the next question is: Is there any advantage in knowing how to solve this or any other problem correctly? Yes, many!

In the first place, it requires judgment and consideration to do anything which has a constructive principle; and those who are most expert and conversant with it are entitled to more respect and better wages than others who never think at all.

But, to say nothing of either respect or reward, there is a positive satisfaction in knowing that we have the ability and power to do and act when called upon.

Now, my young friends, if you wish to be skilful and expert workmen, look to this matter, and by all means endeavor to make yourselves thoroughly conversant with the teachings already given, and those that are to follow.

The model having been examined, lay it in its original position, in order that we may explain its construction, which is shown at

Fig. 2. Here draw any line for a base, as that of A B; now determine on slant of sides which the work is to have, say B C; take any point on A B, as D; draw through it square with A B, cutting at C; square down from B; take C as centre and B radius; draw the circle cutting at E; draw from it parallel with D B, cutting at F; join it and C; this gives bevel W to apply on face of sides, as shown on model. We now want a bevel to apply across the edges of stuff for mitres. It is found by making D A equal D B; take D as centre, and for radius a circle touching B C, cutting at L; join it and A, and we have bevel X for mitres. It is understood that edges of stuff are to be square.

Here it may be mentioned that this same construction gives the cuts for sides and edges of hoppers or boxes. It also gives the side and down cut for purlins, or any kind of framing which stands on a slant, the base of work being square.

PLATE 16.

ROOFING.

To find the covering of an irregular roof; also lengths and cuts of hips and rafters.

This problem is of equal importance to the carpenter as well as the metal plate-worker. Let us suppose that the covering is to be sheet copper, which is not unusual for roofing. Then it is evident that some positive rule must be known before any attempt is made at cutting the material, otherwise the waste would be enormous; besides, the work could not be satisfactory and might be justly condemned.

Here, however, is given a construction which is plain and simple that obviates all difficulties. It is a rule that any one can understand. It not only gives the covering, but the lengths and cuts of every rafter.

The irregular ground plan of this building is shown by the letters A B C D. The covering of roof is now spread out, the drawing being on card-board and already cut, so that you may lift the piece and fold the covering from you. Bring cuts E R and A W together; let the piece in the form of a wedge fall level. Here we have an exact model of the roof; its sides are out of wind; its heights are equal; its hips are regular. Nothing can be more satisfactory than this; it is a self-evident and practical fact before us. Such being the case, then, it is clear that the same rules which produced this model will also give lengths of hip, jack, and common rafters, and all the bevels for cuts.

Replace the model in its original position, and let us explain the construction, as follows:

In the first place bisect angles A B, and through intersections thus made draw seat of hip-rafters meeting at L; draw from it parallel with A D and B C; take any point on line D C, as Y; draw from it square with D C; make Y K equal Y L on the left; draw through K, parallel with D C, cutting lines from L at K H; join D K and C H. These are seats of hip-rafters.

Now determine on rise of roof, say N T; this gives T P for length of rafters between hips L H and L K on both sides of roof. The same length answers between H K, because Y K is equal to N P or Y L on the left; make the rise of hips at L K H equal rise of roof, as N T.

Now find the covering for side B C, and end C D by drawing from L H K square with B C; make P V equal P T; draw through V parallel with B C, cutting lines from L H at F and J; join F B and J C. This completes covering for side B C.

To find the covering for end D C, take C as centre, and with any radius draw the circle shown; make it measure equal on each side of C J; this gives a point, as X, through which draw from C; make C R equal C D; draw from J parallel with C R; make J E equal K H; join E R; make 2 3 equal K T; join 2 J and 2 F. This completes covering for one side and end.

To find the covering for side A D, and end A B; draw from L K, square with A D; make L S equal L F; draw from S parallel with A D, cutting at O; join it and D, also S A.

Now find the covering for end A B by taking B F as radius; with same radius, take S for centre, draw the arc of a circle at W; take A as centre, and B radius; intersect the arc at W, thus giving a point; which join with A S. This completes the covering; its accuracy having already been tested by the model, which would not have come together had there been any error in the construction.

The covering, of course, gives bevels for side cuts of jack-rafters. For example, bevel 4 is side cut for rafters on each side of hip C J, its seat being C H. Again bevel 5 is the side cut for rafters which come against each side of hip that stand over seat D K; and bevel 6 gives side cut of rafters on both sides of hip that stand over seat A L; then bevel 7 gives side cut for rafters which come against both sides of hip that stand over seat B L; lastly, the bevels for down and foot cut of all the rafters are the same as that for common rafter P T; hip-rafters not included.

The angles which they make contain these bevels. It has, we think, been shown that the carpenter and metal plate-worker are equally interested in the solution of this and similar problems, which clearly teach and explain every difficult point by means of card-board models; it is the only way that will satisfy any inquiring mind who wishes to know the reason why.

Plate 16.

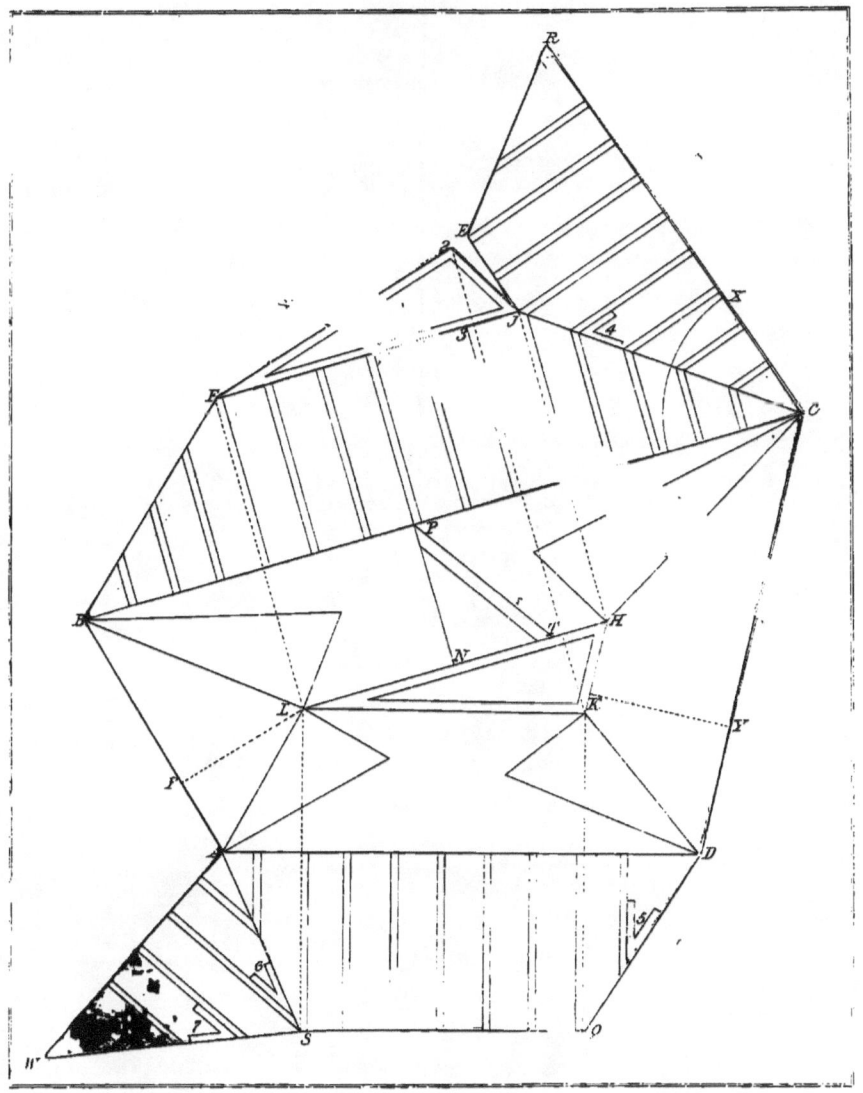

Plate 17.

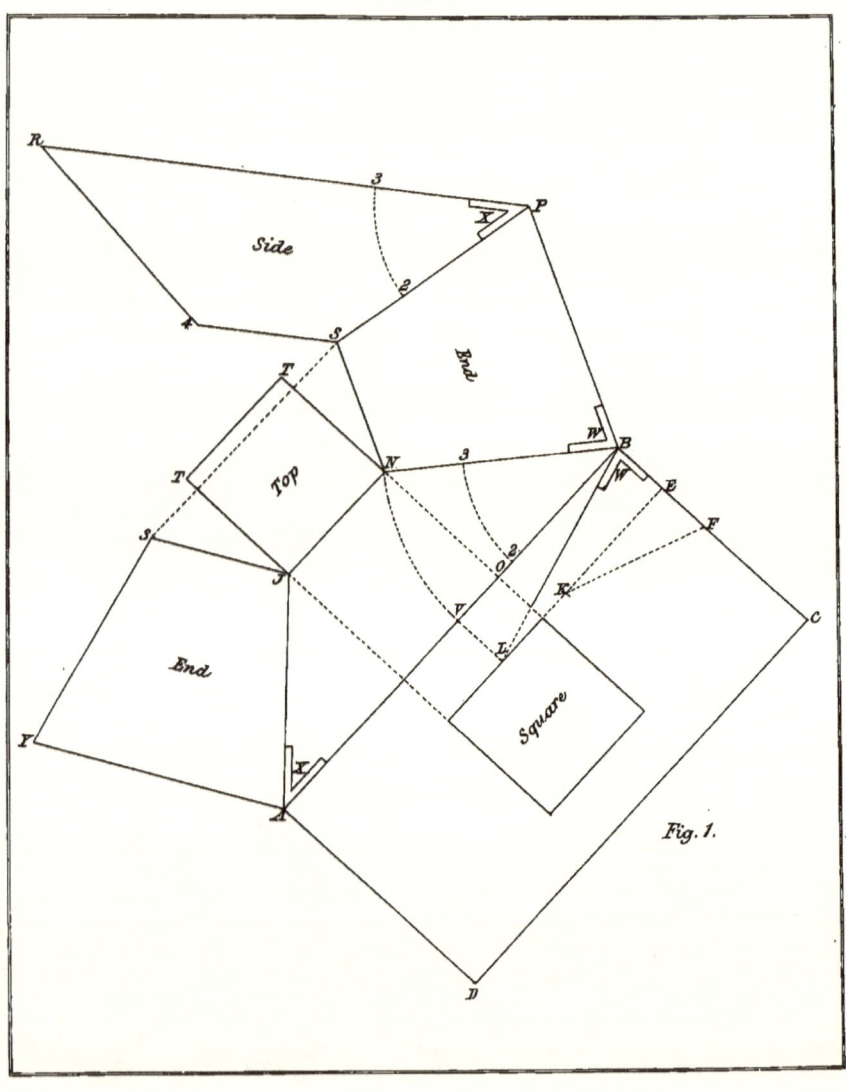

Fig. 1.

PLATE 17.

CONSTRUCTION OF AN OBLONG WITH SLANTING SIDES.

FIGURE 1. The letters A B C D show an oblong base which is to have slanting sides; these, when together at the top, form a square of any given size, as that shown on base.

Now, it is very evident by this arrangement that sides and ends must stand on different slants; in other words, let us suppose a metal or wooden box, with oblong bottom, slanting sides and ends, and the top square. If the material is to be metal, then the whole work may be cut out of one sheet, which means bottom, sides, and top all connected. This understood, the construction is as follows:

Extend upper side of square, cutting at E on the right; make E F equal E B. Now determine on perpendicular height of sides and ends, say E K; join K F; make O N equal K F, square over N J, join J A and N B: this gives one side of the work. Next find slant of ends by making B V equal B N, square down from V to L, join L B: this gives bevel W as the cut for ends. The bevel being reversed and applied as shown, gives a direction to draw B P, which make equal B C; draw from N parallel with B P, make N S equal one side of top as N T,

join S P; draw from S parallel with N J; make S T on the left equal S T on the right; join S J; draw from A parallel with J S; make A Y equal A D; join Y S. This completes one side and both ends.

To find the side which stands on the base D C. Take bevel X, already given, and apply it as shown at P; or take B for centre, and with any radius draw the circle 2.3; with same radius and P centre, draw 2.3; make both circles equal; draw from P through 3; make P R equal A B; draw from S parallel with P R; make S 4 equal S N; join 4 R. This completes sides, ends, and top.

To have a correct idea of this construction, let the drawing be made on card-board; then cut it clear through all the outer lines. This done, make side and base work on a hinge by a slight cut on line A B; make a similar cut on A J and B N; also on P S and N J.

Now lift the piece and fold its sides and ends from you; bring the joints R 4 and S Y together; make the top fall level, and we have a perfect model of the work.

PLATE 18.

FIGURE 1 shows the elbow of a hollow pipe standing at a right angle. The object here is to give the form of sheet-metal for mitre-joints of pipes.

This problem being nothing more than that of finding the covering of a cylinder which has been cut obliquely.

To understand this is just as much the business of a carpenter as a metal-plate worker — both are equally interested.

The construction is quite simple, and is as follows:

Fig. 2 shows the base of a hollow pipe, its diameter being A B. It is now required to find the shape of two pieces of sheet-metal which, being rolled and connected, will form a mitre-joint, as that of Fig. 1. ·

To do this, square up from B; make B C equal B A; join C A; divide the semicircle into any number of equal parts, as six; draw through each part square with diameter, cutting it and line A C. This done, come to Fig. 3. Here draw any line, as L K; take any point on it, say B; set off on each side of it six equal parts, each to equal one of those on semicircle, Fig. 2; square up all the divisions on line L K; make B C equal B C, Fig. 2; make all the heights on each side of B C equal corresponding heights and letters at Fig. 2. This done, trace through the points a curved line, as shown, and we have an exact pattern by which the metal is cut, making two pieces, as that of Fig. 3 and Fig. 4; these being rolled into pipes, the edges form mitre-joints, and these being brought together and fastened, form the elbow standing at a right angle.

It is easy to have a practical illustration of this by having the drawing on card-board, which cut and roll in the manner stated, and the result is a model of the pipe or two sections of a cylinder cut obliquely.

It will be noticed that parts of the curve may be struck from centres, as shown.

·

54

Plate 18.

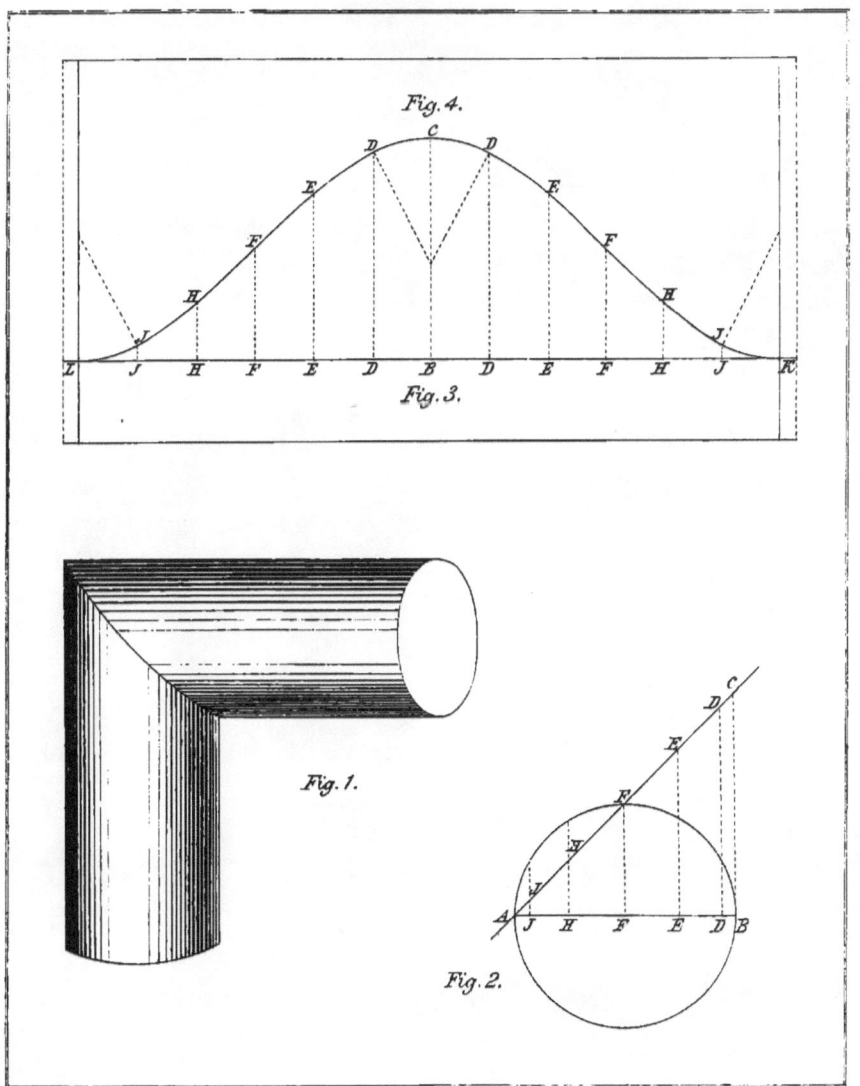

Fig. 4.

Fig. 3.

Fig. 1.

Fig. 2.

Plate 19.

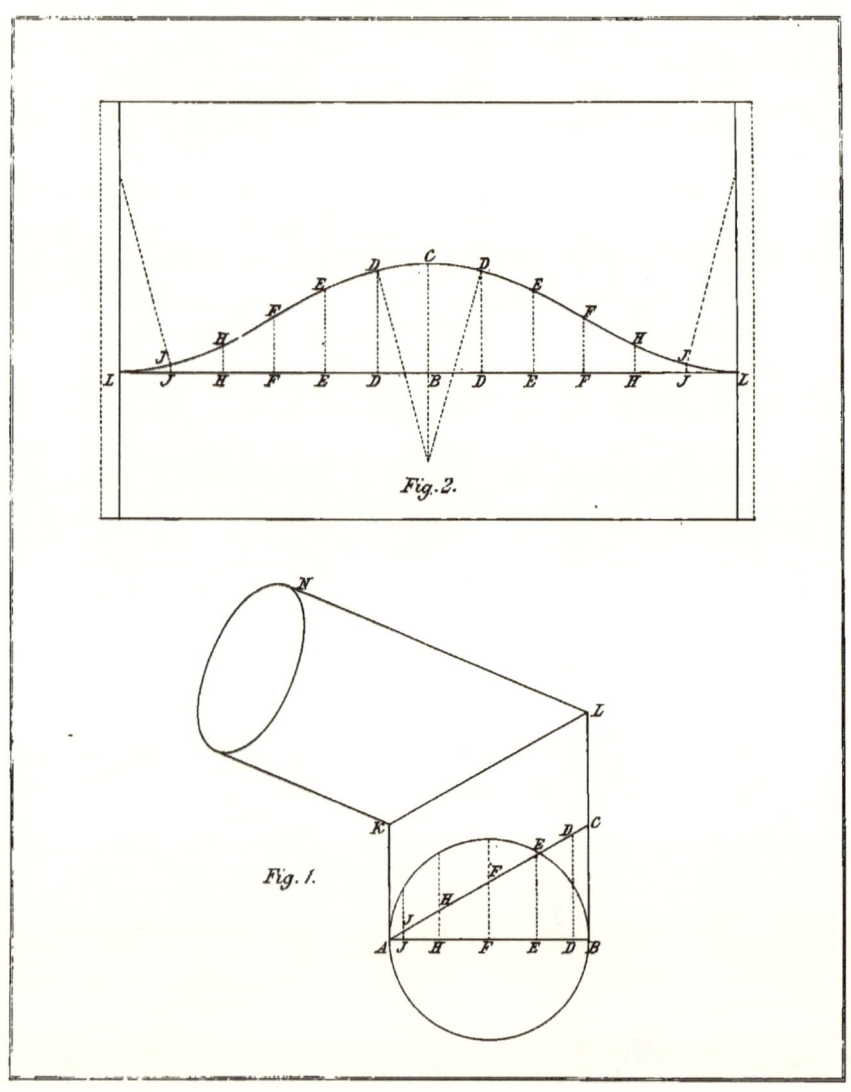

Fig. 2.

Fig. 1.

PLATE 19.

SECTIONS OF HOLLOW PIPES.

FIGURE 1. To find the form of sheet-metal for mitre-joint of a hollow pipe standing at any angle. Here it will be noticed that this construction is almost similar to that given on preceding plate. The same rule applies to all angles, on condition that the pipe is parallel, and of equal diameter at each end, as in this case.

The assumed angle here is B L N, and the mitre-joint L K. The diameter of pipe being A B; draw A C parallel with K L; divide the semicircle into any number of equal parts, say six; draw through each part square with diameter cutting it and line A C. This done, come to Fig. 2. Here draw any line, as L L; take any point on it, as B; set off on each side of it six parts, each to equal one of those on semicircle, Fig. 1. Square up lines from each division on L L; now make B C equal B C, Fig. 1; also make all heights on each side of B C equal corresponding heights and letters of Fig. 1. Thus points are given through which trace the curved line.

Here it will be observed that parts of this curve may be struck from centres, as shown.

We have now a pattern by which the metal is marked and cut, thus giving two pieces having curved edges, which form mitres when the metal is rolled into pipes; these being connected, form the angle B L N, Fig. 1.

The practical solution of this problem may be had by cutting a piece of paper to curved line, as drawn. The cut making two pieces, roll these into the form of pipes; bring the mitres together, and we have the model of an elbow, making the required angle B L N. The dotted lines from L L on right and left, are overlaps for sheet-metal.

PLATE 20.

HOLLOW PIPE IN THREE SECTIONS.

FIGURE 1. To construct a pattern by which sheet-metal may be cut to form the elbow of a pipe in three or more sections. The solution of this problem differs but little, if any, from those already given. The three pieces of pipe may be considered as three sections of a cylinder which have been cut obliquely, each piece in the form of a blunt *wedge;* these, on being brought together, form a solid elbow, which shows the problem to be nothing more than that of finding the covering of sections cut in the manner just stated. This is done by the following rule:

Draw any line as 2 P parallel with diameter A B of pipe; take any point as P, and draw the quadrant 2 N, which divide into four equal parts; draw from P through each part, square up from 2, cutting K; then square over from N, cutting L; join it and K; draw A C parallel with P K, divide semicircle A B into six parts; draw through each part square with diameter A B, cutting it and line A C.

Now come to Fig. 2. Here draw any line as that of L L; take any point on it as B; draw through it square with L L; set off on each side of B six parts, each to equal one of those on semicircle, Fig. 1; make L K on right and left equal K L, Fig. 1; join K K: this done, square up divisions as shown from line L L, cutting line K K; make B C equal B C, Fig. 1; also make all heights on each side of B C, above line L L, equal corresponding heights and letters at Fig. 1.

Points are now given, indicated by letters, through which trace the curve for pattern; this being cut, turn it over; keep line L L on that of K K. Now mark curve K V K, thus giving Figs. 2, 3, 4 as the shape of three pieces of sheet-metal; these, rolled into pipes, are three sections which form the elbow. Here notice that the distance C V, at Fig. 3, is equal to R V, at Fig. 1, and, further, observe that parts of curve may be struck from centres.

Plate 20.

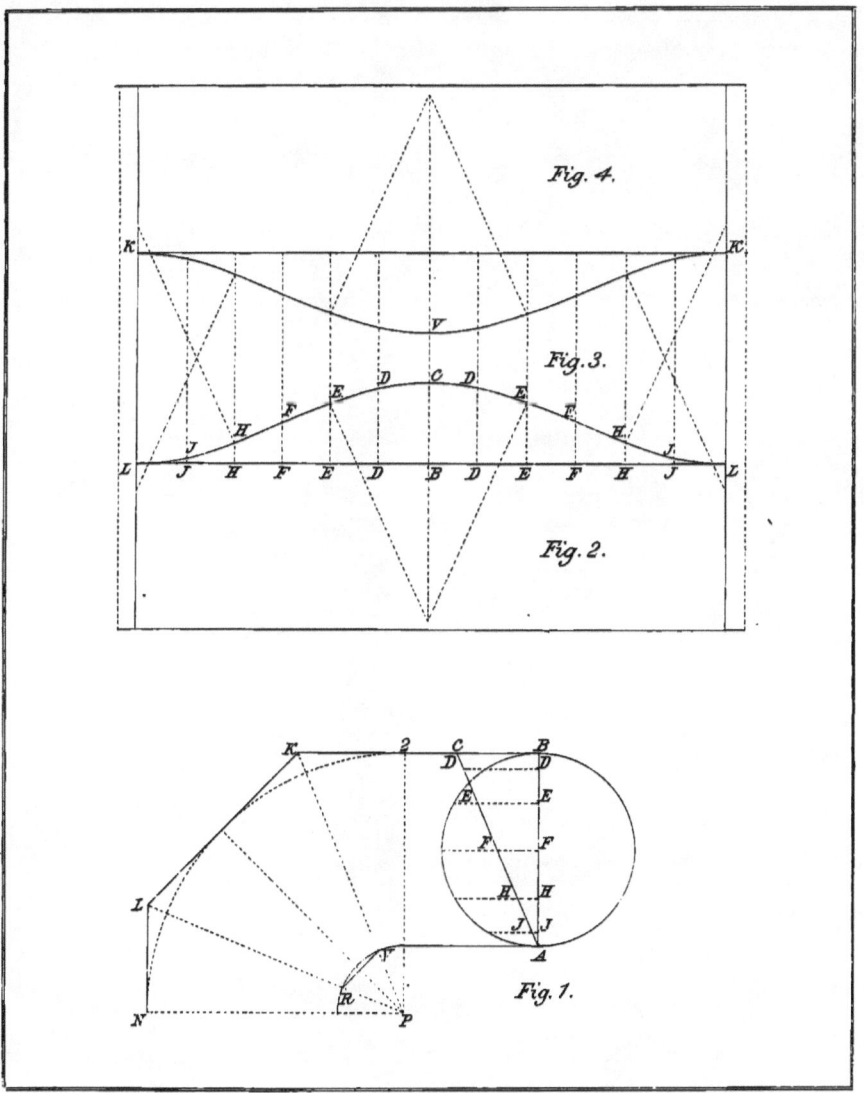

Fig. 4.

Fig. 3.

Fig. 2.

Fig. 1.

Plate 21.

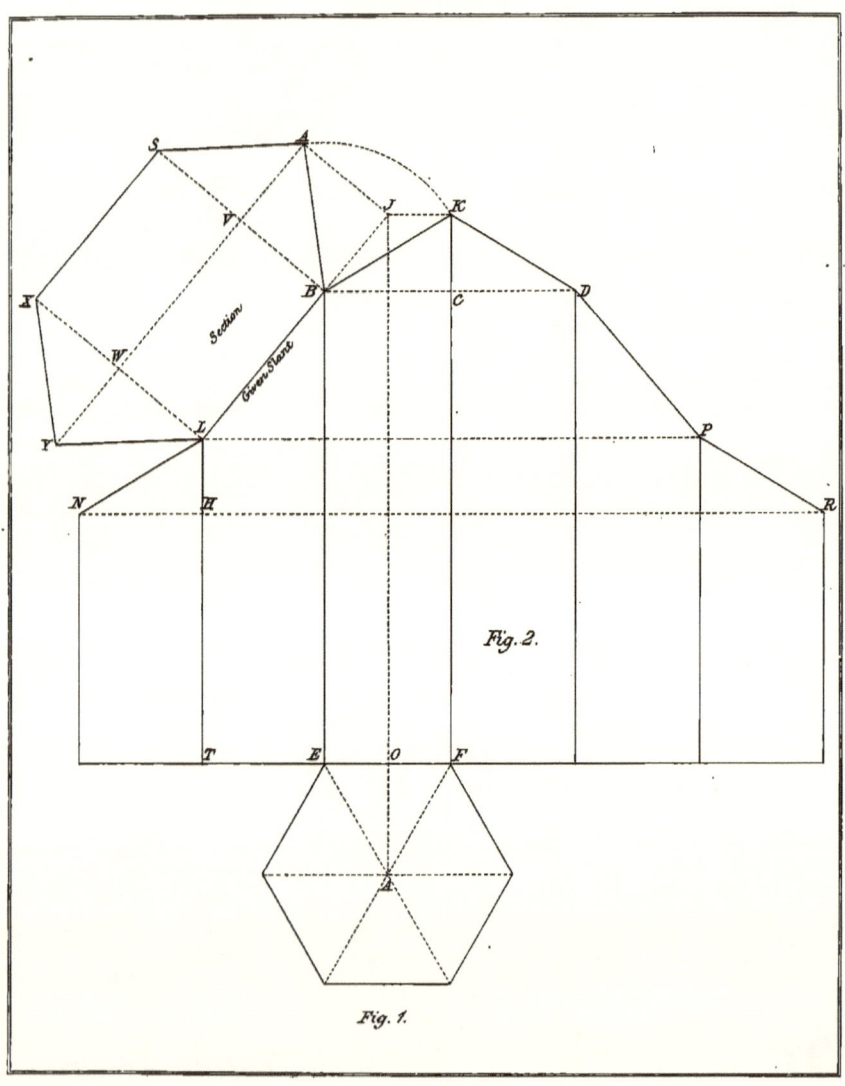

Section

Cover Slant

Fig. 2.

Fig. 1.

PLATE 21.

THE PRISM AND ITS SECTION.

To find the section of a hexagon prism which has been cut obliquely to any angle not parallel with its base. The meaning and use of this problem will be best understood by having the drawing on cardboard, which, being cut as directed, will form an exact model of a prism and its section. The construction is as follows:

Fig. 1 is the base, and Fig. 2 shows six sides of the base unfolded or spread out. Take one of the sides as T E, and draw on the upper part of it any given slant, say L B; extend this line; then draw a line from A, Fig. 1, cutting the slant at J; square over from it cutting at K; draw from B and L parallel with J K, cutting at D and P on the right; join B K and K D P; this done, make L H on the left equal C K above; draw through H, cutting at N and R; join R P on the right and N L on the

left; now draw from L B J square with slant; this done, make J A equal O A at the base; draw A Y parallel with slant; make W Y equal V A and make V S equal V B; draw S X; now join X Y L and S A B. This completes the section, and shows its exact form as made by the cut through L B, which is on one side of the prism.

Let us now produce the model by cutting clear through all the outer lines; make the section work on a hinge by a slight cut on line L B, and in like manner cut the base on line E F. Also a slight cut on each line representing the sides, in order that *they* may work on a hinge. This being done, lift the piece and fold its sides against the base, and make the section rest on the sides; thus a model is formed by means of a simple construction which should be known by metal-plate workers and others.

PLATE 22.

THE ELLIPSE AND SECTIONS OF SOLIDS.

FIGURE 1 shows a method to describe the semi-ellipse from three centres. Here it may be observed that this or a similar figure cannot be drawn correctly by means of compasses; and yet it is near enough for many practical purposes, and in some cases it is even preferable to the exact figure, as will be shown presently.

Here the long diameter is given as A B, which divide at C; draw through it square with A B; assume C D as the rise; square up from A; make it and E equal C D; divide A E at N; join it and D; divide A C at H; join it and E, cutting line N D at V. Now bisect V D, and draw through intersections thus made, cutting at O; join it and E. This line, having cut long diameter at L, gives it for a centre. Make B P on the right equal A L, and we have O L P as three points or centres from which the curves are struck, as shown.

The figure just drawn is a near approximate to being correct, and we shall use it, as above stated, for several constructions yet to follow.

Fig. 2 is the base of a cylinder inclosed by a square. The object here is to show that if a cylinder is cut obliquely, its section must be elliptical; and, on the other hand, if the oblique cut B C is through a square prism, its section must be a rectangle or oblong. But to have a clear perception of this, the learner is advised to use card-board: it being cut and folded as directed, gives a model by which everything is understood at a glance. To do this, set off from R two sides of the square and one from P on the left; this done, square up sides of prism, as shown; take any point on line from P, say A; draw from it parallel with P R, cutting at A on the right. Now assume the slant or oblique cut as B C; make A B on the right equal A B on the left; join B F; draw from B and C square with slant; make C E equal C A; draw from E parallel with slant, cutting at S; this gives B C E S as the section of a square prism made by slant cut B C. It is also clear that if a cylinder is cut in like manner, its section must be the elliptical figure shown. This will be quite evident by cutting the card clear through all the outer lines of the drawing, and making a slight cut on lines B C and P R. In order to form a hinge for each piece, make a slight cut on line P A B, and in like manner on R C, also K F. Now lift the piece and fold its sides on square base, turn the section on its hinge B C until line E S rests on cut F B, and we have the model of a square prism, also its section and that of a cylinder made by cut B C.

This illustration, being on card-board, conveys more instruction to the mind of the learner, as to what is meant by the sections of solids, than any other means. In our own experience, we have found the card-board to possess every advantage over the old "wooden block" system. The material is inexpensive and readily obtained; it is quite manageable, requiring simply a knife to cut, and in cutting it forms its own hinges. In fact, its entire superiority occasions surprise that so simple and clean a substitute has not been generally adopted long since.

Plate 22.

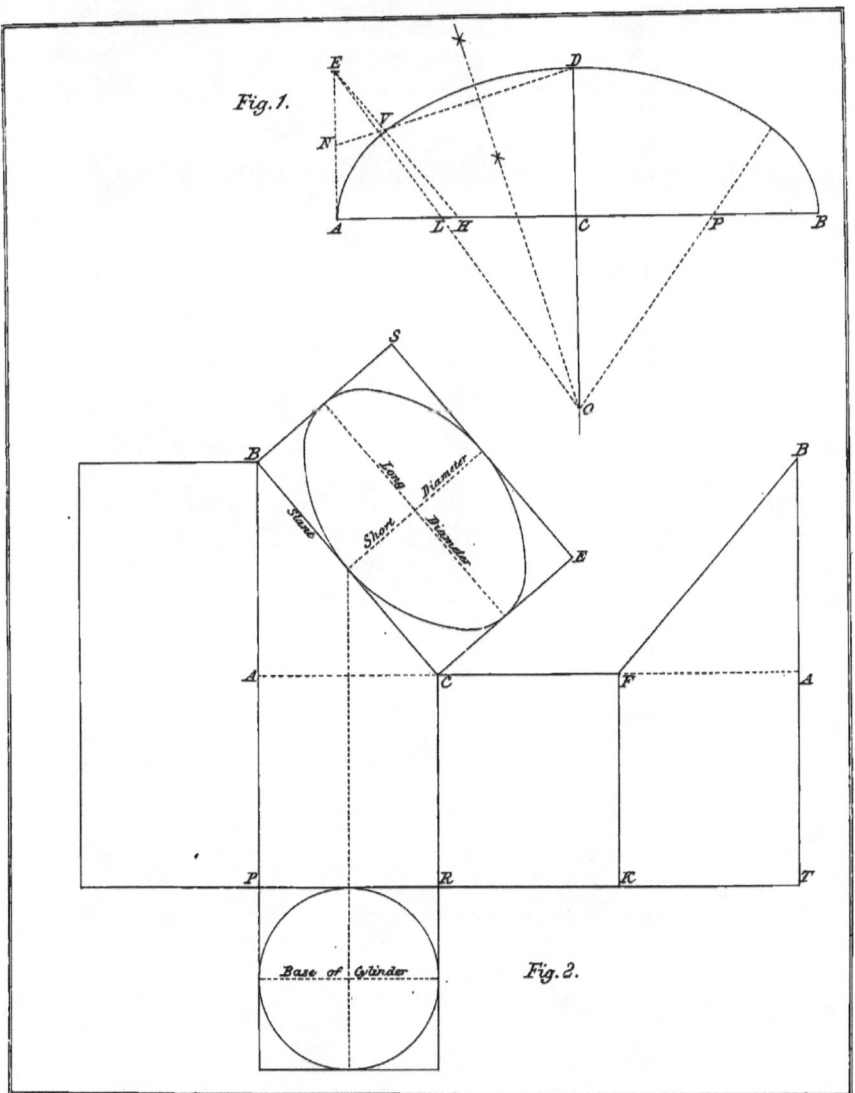

Fig.1.

E D
V
N
A L H C P B

S
B
Long Diameter
Stone Short Diameter
E

B

A C F A

P R K T

Base of Cylinder

Fig.2.

Plate 23.

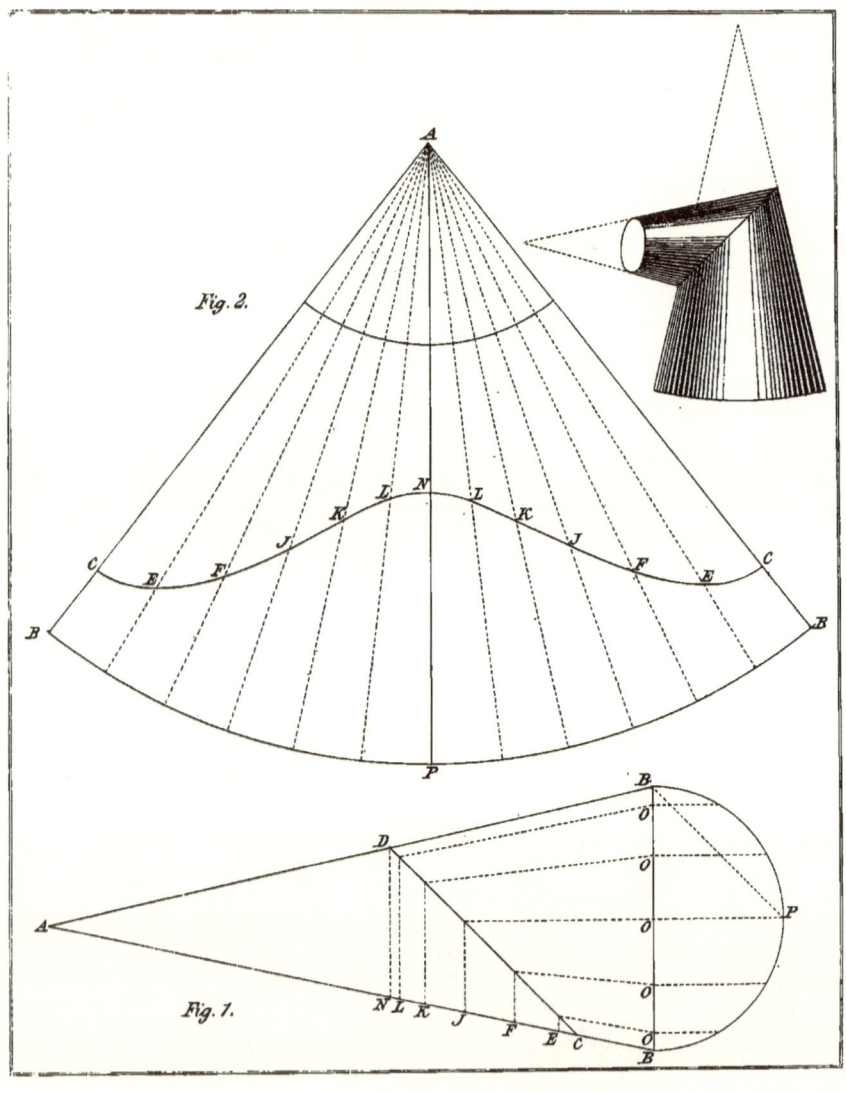

Fig. 2.

Fig. 1.

PLATE 23.

SECTIONS OF HOLLOW CONES.

To find the mitre-joint for a tapering pipe similar to figure shown on upper part of plate to the right. The only difference in this construction from previous plates is, that here the pipe may be considered a hollow cone, for which we are to find a covering; and also show the form of a curve that will make a mitre-joint for an elbow. This we can readily do by the following method:

Fig. 1. The semicircle on the right shows half the base of pipe, its diameter being B B. Assume the taper as meeting in point A. Now determine on angle of mitre, say forty-five degrees, which is that of B P on semicircle. The next question is the portion of pipe where the elbow mitres, say line C D, which is parallel with that of B P; divide the semicircle into any number of parts, as six; draw from each part square with diameter B B, cutting it at points O O O O O, and from each of these draw in the direction of point A, cutting line C D, and from which intersections draw parallel with B B, cutting slant A B at N L K J, etc.

Now come to Fig. 2. Here draw any line, as A P; make it equal A B, Fig. 1; take A as centre and P as radius; draw the curve through P; set off on each side of P six parts; make each part equal one of those on semicircle, Fig. 1; this done, draw from A, cutting at each point on curve through P, ending at B on right and left, which is equal to the circumference of pipe at its base; make A C on right and left equal A C at Fig. 1; again make A F E equal A F E, Fig. 1. Continue in this manner until points are found, through which trace the curve as shown, and we have a pattern to cut the sheet-metal by; it making two pieces, which, being rolled, form two pieces of tapering pipe with mitres: these being connected form the elbow, as stated.

71

PLATE 24.

TO FIND THE CURVES OF BOARDS OR METAL FOR COVERING A DOME.

To make a pattern by which metal or boards may be cut for covering a spherical "dome." Each piece of covering having its edges curved, and terminate in a point. To do this, divide the base of dome, or one-quarter of it, into any number of courses that will suit the metal or boards. The method is as follows:

Fig. 1 shows the elevation of dome, as A B C. We now want a straight line which shall equal the curve C B. Take C as centre and L as radius; intersect the curve at E; join *it* and L; draw from B parallel with E L, cutting at D; then D C is equal to curve C B.

Fig. 2. Here have a board of sufficient length for a pattern, and at any convenient place draw a quar- ter circle as shown; let its radius N P equal half the width of board for pattern; this means, at the base; here divide the curve N P into any number of equal parts, say four; and in like manner divide N N into four parts; draw from these through divisions on quarter circle, giving 2.2 3.3 4.4; this done, run a line through the board as C B; make it equal C D in Fig. 1; divide C B into four equal parts, through which draw 2.2 3.3 4.4 parallel and equal with cor- responding distances and figures at quarter circle; thus giving points for nails as a guide to bend a strip, by which the curve is marked. The same applica- tion to opposite side gives a similar curve: then the board being worked to both curves completes the pattern.

Plate 24.

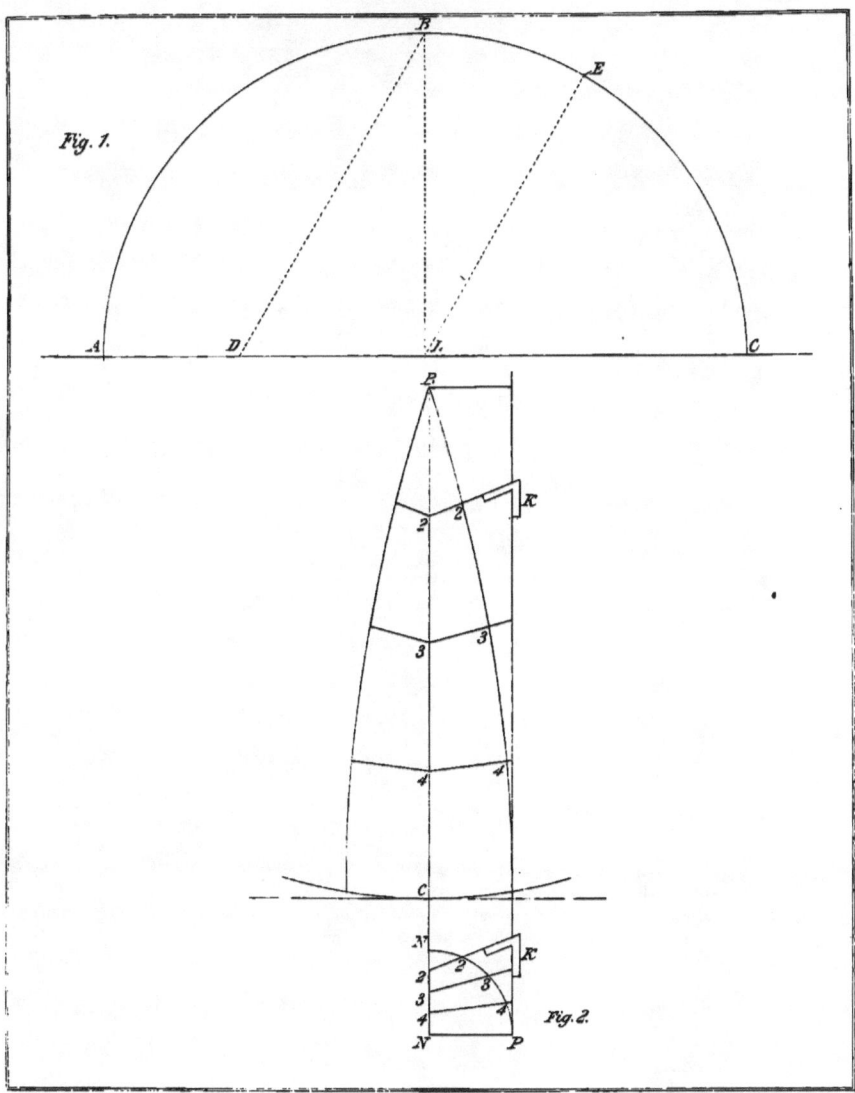

Fig. 1.

Fig. 2.

Plate 25.

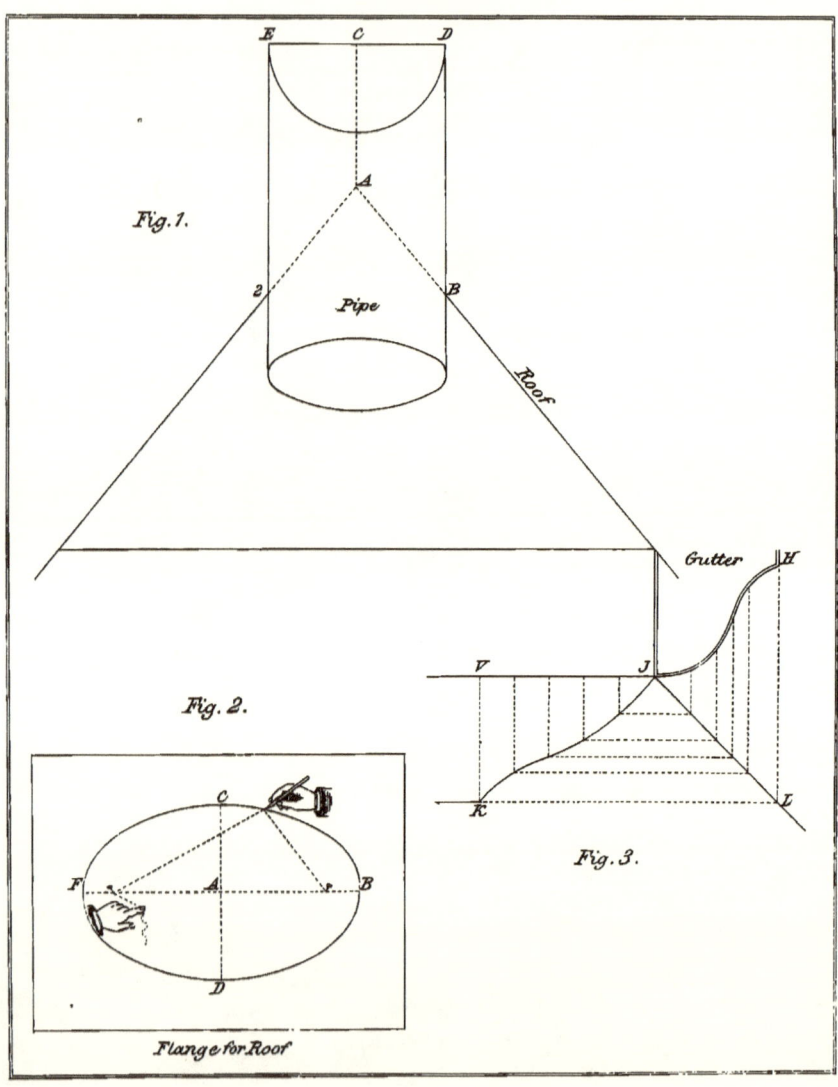

Fig. 1.

E C D

A

2 Pipe B

Roof

Fig. 2.

Gutter H

V J

K L

Fig. 3.

C

F A B

D

Flange for Roof

PLATE 25.

A HOLLOW PIPE PASSING THROUGH A ROOF.

FIGURE 1. To find the aperture or opening of a *flange* in sheet-metal, which shall fit both pitches of a roof, and receive a circular pipe passing through the roof, and stand perpendicular. Its diameter being E D and its radius C D. Draw from D parallel with C A, cutting the roof at B; then A B is half the long diameter of an ellipse.

We now want a piece of *flat* sheet-metal; this is shown at Fig. 2. Here draw any two lines at right angles; make A B and A F each equal A B on roof, Fig. 1; also make D A C equal E C D, Fig. 1.

We are now ready to strike the curves with a string. This method has been already explained, but here it may be repeated, and in this way : take A B as radius; with same radius take C for centre, and intersect long diameter to left of B and right of F. These are points that may be punched to receive pins. Tie a string to that on the right, bring it around the pin on the left; now sweep the curve, as shown. This being done, cut out the ellipse; then bend the flange on its short diameter, D C, until it forms an angle to equal that of 2 A B on the roof; this done, the pipe will be found to fit the opening which has been cut through the flange.

Fig. 3. To find on the flat surface of sheet-metal the form of a mitre-joint for a curved gutter, as that of H J, which is to return on the corner of a building at right angles. To do this, set off from H to J any number of equal parts on curve, say five; set off the same number from J, ending at V; now draw from each part square with J V, and in like manner draw from each part on curve, cutting mitre-line J L; thus points are given on J L, from which draw, cutting the lines from J V, and through intersections thus made draw the curved line from K to J; then a pattern being made to this line gives the mitre-joint for gutter.

PLATE 26.

FIGURE 1 shows a small pipe on a slant entering a main one standing upright. The diameter A X enters side of main pipe at points A and X. Now proceed and find a straight line that will equal one-quarter circumference of main pipe. To do this, take P as centre and H radius; intersect the circle at V; join it and H; draw from N parallel with V H, cutting at R; then R P equals one-quarter of the circumference; this done, make H 2 equal half diameter of small pipe; draw from 2 square with P H, cutting at 3; this gives L 3 as half the opening on surface of main pipe for small one.

Fig. 2. Here is shown a surface of sheet-metal for main pipe. Draw any two lines at right angles, cutting at point O; make O Y and O W on right and left equal double the distance P R on diameter of main pipe; make O L on right and left equal 3 L, the curve on main pipe; this done, make O A and O X equal D X on side of main pipe, Fig. 1. The drawing being completed, we place the main pipe in position,—standing upright,—and it becomes clear that the line A X is the long diameter of an ellipse, and L O L, the short diameter, stands level. Now the ellipse being cut through, the metal is rolled, and forms the main pipe, and the elliptic opening on its surface is ready to receive the small slanting pipe, as shown at Fig. 1. The dotted lines on right of Y and left of W indicate a lap for riveting.

To find on a flat surface the shape of metal for small pipe, we now return to Fig. 1. Here divide the semicircle from A to X into any number of equal parts, say six; draw through each part parallel with X X, cutting diameter and side of main pipe.

Now come to Fig. 3. Here draw the right angles as A A and X X; set off on each side of X six parts, each to equal one of those on semicircle at Fig. 1; square up the parts from line A A, and make X X equal X X, Fig. 1. Now on each side of X, on line A A, make heights equal to corresponding heights and letters at Fig. 1; points are thus given, through which trace the curve, as shown. The metal being rolled, forms the small pipe; its end, which has been cut to the curve, will be found to enter or fit opening in main pipe.

Plate 26.

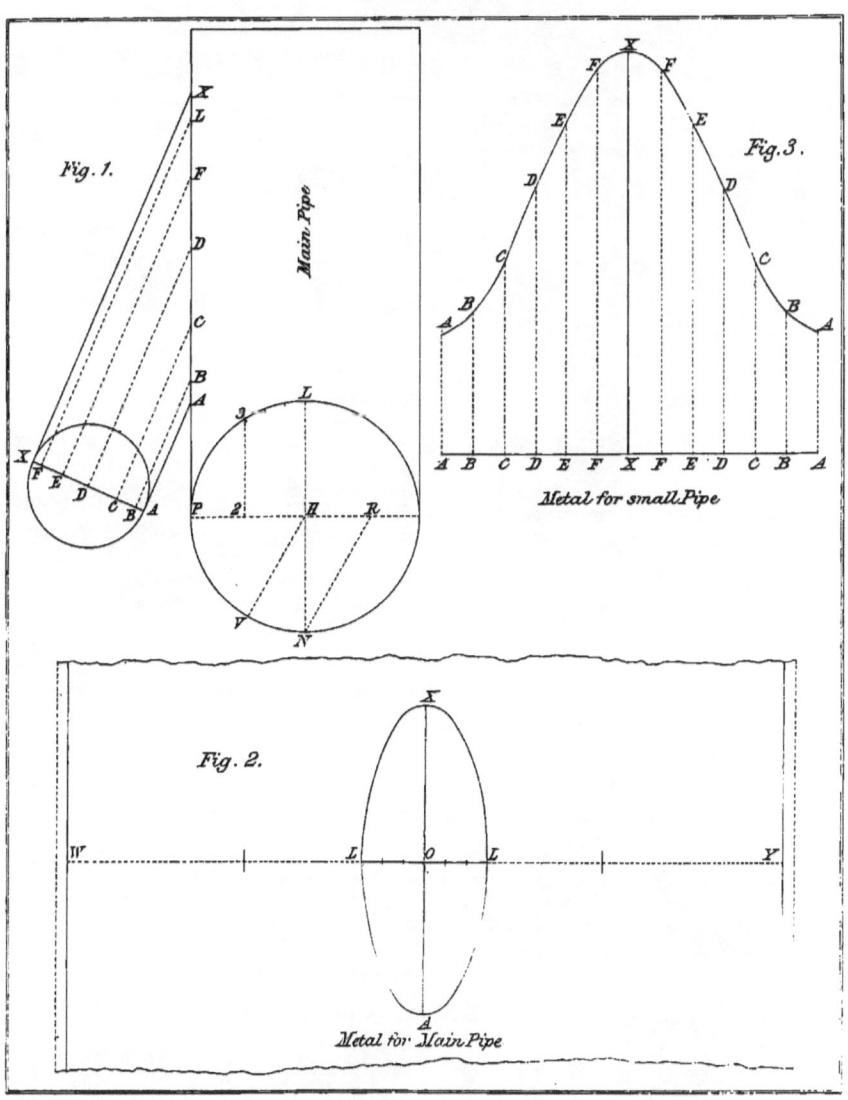

Fig. 1.

Main Pipe

Fig. 3.

Metal for small Pipe

Fig. 2.

Metal for Main Pipe

Plate 27.

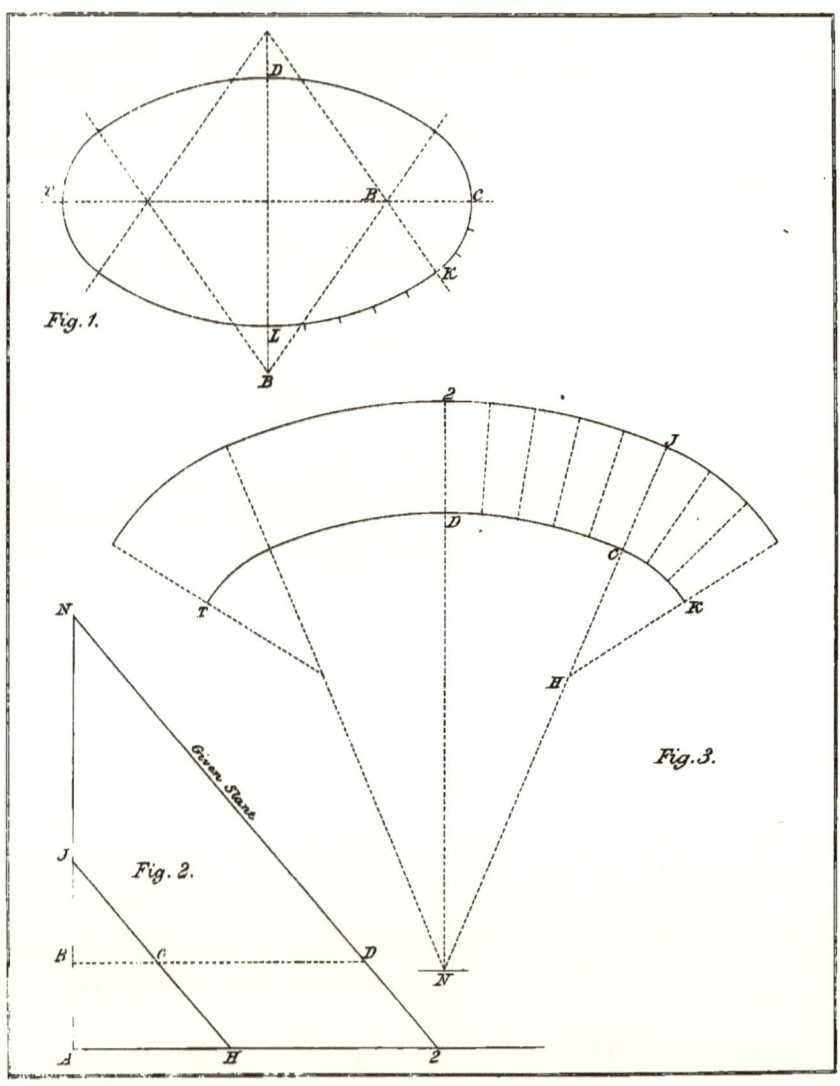

Fig. 1.

Fig. 2.

Given Slant

Fig. 3.

PLATE 27.

TO CONSTRUCT SLANTING SIDES FOR AN ELLIPTICAL BASE.

FIGURE 1 represents an elliptical figure, which may be considered either a base or a bottom, around which is to stand a side of any width, and incline to any angle.

This problem and its solution is of equal value to the joiner, mason, and metal-plate worker.

Let us give some idea of its use and practical application. For example, it is required to construct a splayed arch, its form to be elliptical, and its edges come flush with straight walls. This statement shows that the arch must have two unequal curves, because its face is on the same splay at the crown and at the springing. To accomplish this might seem a very difficult task. Such, however, is not the case. We have only to look around and see a tinsmith cutting his metal for a boiler, or anything having an oval bottom and slanting sides. The rule that he applies to his work also applies, without the slightest deviation, to the perfect construction of a splayed arch, or any work which bends and stands on a slant.

Let us now explain the simple method by which is found a slanting side for semi-ellipse as T D C, which is one-half the figure shown. Come to Fig. 2. Here form a right angle; take A 2 for a base. Now determine the perpendicular height of side above the base, say A B; draw from B parallel with A 2;

make B C equal B C, Fig. 1; again, make B D equal B D, Fig. 1; this done, draw through D any slant desired for side of work, say line N 2; now draw through C parallel with N 2, cutting at H and J.

We are now ready to give the curves on edges of side, as shown at Fig. 3. Here draw any perpendicular line as that of 2 D N, which make equal with 2 D N, Fig. 2. Take N as centre, and draw the curves through D and C; this done, come to Fig. 1, and divide L K into any number of equal parts, say five; with one of these return to Fig. 3, and set off from D five parts, ending in C; draw from N through C; now make C H equal C J, Fig. 2; take H as centre, and draw the curves from C and J. Come again to Fig. 1, and divide K C into any number of equal parts, say three; return with one of these, and set off from C three parts, ending in K; draw from H through K; make curves on left of D 2 equal those on the right. This completes one slanting side; and if it were cut through the paper as now drawn, and its curved edge, T D K, made to stand on T D C, Fig. 1, then both its edges will be found perfectly level, and the face or surface of side stands on the given slant.

Here we see in this simple construction a complete illustration of the splayed semi-elliptical arch.

83

PLATE 28.

STRAIGHT AND CIRCULAR WORK ON THE SLANT.

FIGURE 1. To construct slanting sides to a base or bottom, parts of which are straight and circular, as that shown.

This problem, like the preceding, applies and gives the cuts and curves for anything standing on a slant. It applies to either wood or metal. It is practical and simple. The plan of work may be either straight or circular. Take, for example, something which is familiar, and similar to the drawing before us, say a seat having a slanting back and circular ends, or such as may be seen in carriages and other vehicles. The edges of a board for this back must be curved, and in a manner that when its ends are bent for quarter circles, that operation at once throws the board on a slant, and its edges, which have been curved, are now level. This might seem simple, which it really is; and yet it has a constructive principle that must be known, in order to find the proper curves for edges of work, which bend and stand on a slant, as is the case here, where we have four quarter circles. Around these and straight parts of the plan are to stand sides on an equal slant, which means that circular corners and straight sides incline alike.

To do this, come to Fig. 2. Here form a right angle; take L N as a base; now determine the perpendicular height of sides, say L A; draw from A parallel with L N; make A B equal A B, Fig. 1; draw through B any slant desired, say line P N; this gives N B for slant width of sides; make B P, Fig. 1, equal B P, Fig. 2; take P as centre and B radius; draw the curve towards C; divide quarter circle B E into any number of equal parts, say five; set off the same from B on the curve, ending at C; draw from P through C; draw from C square with it and P, and make C K equal E H. This completes the inner curve. Now make B N equal the slant width of sides; take P again as centre and N as radius, and draw the outer curve.

This simple construction is now complete. Its accuracy may be tested by having the drawing on card-board, and cut clear through all the outer and inner lines, making the sides on right and left work on a hinge by a slight cut along each line; this being done, lift the piece, fold the straight and circular parts from you; bring the square joints together, and you have an exact model of the work, — its sides and circular corners standing on the given slant.

Here it is understood that the construction just explained applies to either wood or metal.

Plate 28.

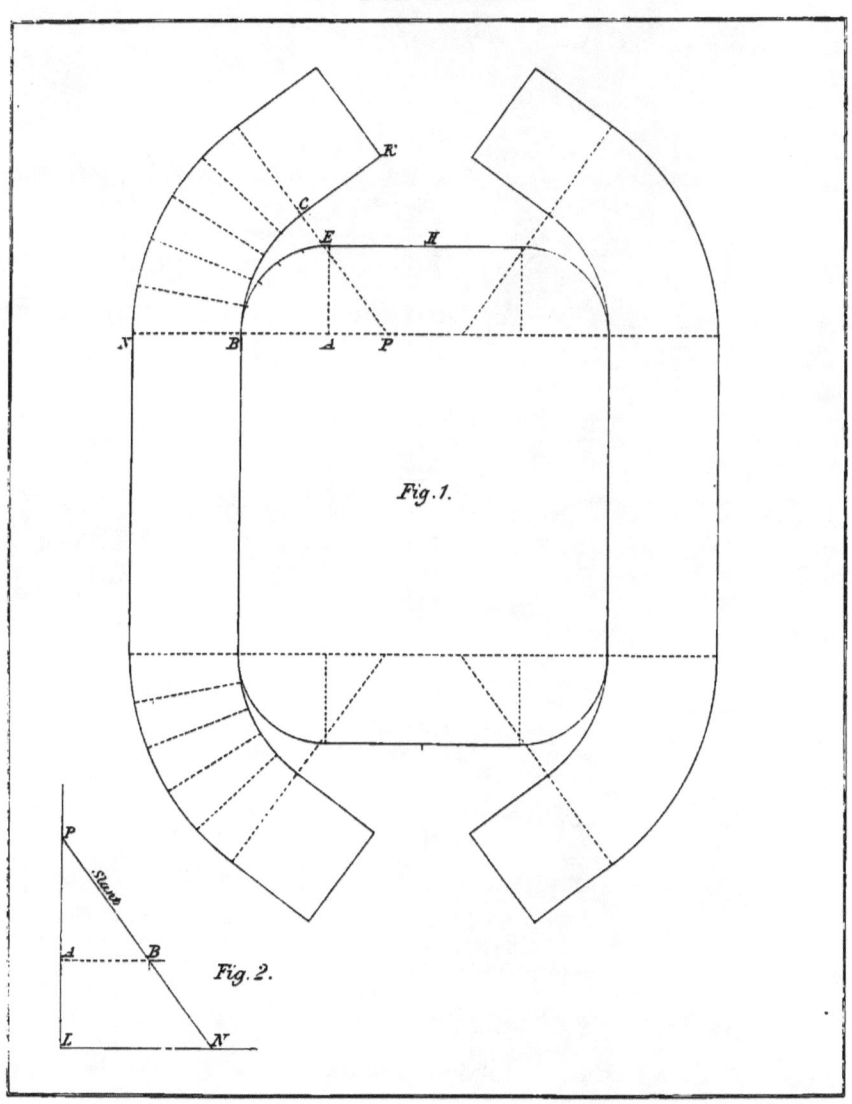

Fig.1.

Fig.2.

Plate 29.

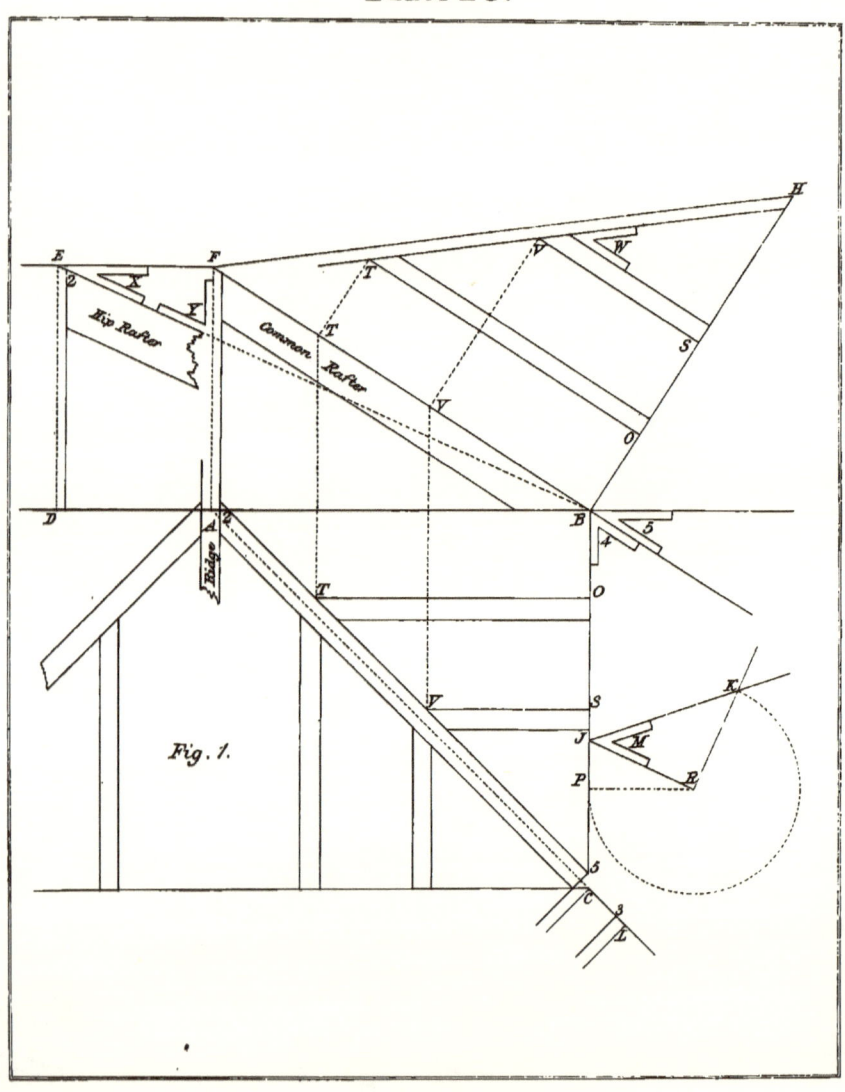

Fig. 1.

PLATE 29.

ROOFING.

FIGURE 1 shows a method by which is found lengths and cuts of jack-rafters for a hip-roof, its angles being square.

The most ready and practical way to do this is to lay down but one angle of the building, and work to a scale, say one and a half inches to the foot. By this means, the length and cut of every rafter are obtained with correctness. Besides, the work is done on the ground much better and quicker than the way which is sometimes adopted, of hoisting timber on the building, and then commence marking, and perhaps guessing as to the proper length or cut of a rafter.

Here the drawing is laid down on the least possible space, and the whole construction given from one angle of the building, as that of A B C; the dotted line C A being the seat of hip, set off on each side of it half thickness of timber for the hip. Now make B D, equal dotted line C A; square up from A and D; this done, determine the rise of roof, say dotted line A F; draw from F parallel with A D, cutting line from D at E; join it and B. This gives E B, as length of hip-rafter, and by drawing F B, we have length of common rafter.

This line also gives bevels 4 and 5 for foot and down cuts of all the rafters; then line E B in like manner gives bevels X and Y for foot and down cut of hip-rafter, so that now we have only to find lengths, and side cut of jack-rafters which come against the hip. This is done by drawing from B square with B F; make B H equal B A; join H F. This is the covering of one hip, and by it is found the length of rafters as follows:

Set off from line H F half thickness of hip, as shown; then set off on ground-plan the position of one or two jack-rafters as those of V T, from which points draw parallel with B C, cutting common rafter at V T, and from these draw parallel with B H, cutting half thickness of hip at V T; thus giving O T and S V, as the length of two rafters, that when in position, will stand exactly over those having corresponding letters on the plan, and bevel W gives the side cut for all rafters which come against the hip. The bevel for down cut has already been given as that of 4.

Here no one can fail seeing with what simplicity and ease the lengths and cuts of rafters have been obtained. Not only this, but it is also a practical, quick, and correct method for any hip-roof where the building makes right angles.

We return to hip-rafter, and find its cut against the ridge, by taking any point on line B C, say J; draw from it parallel with hip B E; now take any point below J, say P; square over from it, cutting at R; draw square from it and J; make R K equal R P; draw from J through K, and we have bevel M for side cut of hip.

Backing the hip seems a useless waste of time for this or similar roofs, because if the hip is shortened to a point, as that of 5, where backing would commence, this is quite sufficient, — in other words, have its edge square. To do this, set off from D half thickness of ridge, and draw solid line, cutting at 2, which gives 2 B; make it and 2 L on seat of hip equal; then the distance between lines from C and 5, being set off from L, gives 3.2 as length of hip-rafter. Thus we avoid the trouble of backing by merely shortening the hip.

PLATE 30.

ROOFING.

To find lengths and cuts of rafters for a hexagon roof.

Fig. 1 is the ground-plan of the building, it having six sides; one of which being projected, by means of it we find, in the most simple manner, the exact length and cut of every rafter in the roof.

Commence by dividing any two sides of plan into equal parts, as that of C D and F E; draw from divisions thus made, square with sides C D and F E, meeting in O as centre; around it form the small hexagon. Draw from L through O; now determine rise of roof, say O B; draw from B through A, and we have the given rafter. Its foot and down cuts are shown by bevels X and Y.

To find the hip-rafter, make O N equal O B; join N L, which gives the hip. Here notice centre of seat, cutting the angle of small hexagon: this would cause a double cut on upper end of hip; but to avoid that, take off the corner, as shown.

The bevels V and P give foot and down cut for all the hips. These perhaps would be better to have a backing, which is found by drawing a line through any part of the seat, and square with L N; draw from the two points of intersection at seat, and square with it, cutting L N from that point, as shown; draw square with O N, cutting line from half thickness of hip. Thus a point is given to draw dotted line, which is the backing required.

To find lengths and side cut of jack-rafters. Draw a line from O square with C D; make 2 B equal A B; join B D C; set off on each side of B C and B D half thickness of hips. Now lay off position of rafters on line C D, draw them parallel with 2 B, cutting the hips, and we have the lengths; also bevel W for side cuts. The down and foot cuts are the same as given rafter.

Here is seen that every rafter, hip, and cut for this roof, is obtained by the most simple means. It is also clear that by working to a scale, say one and a half inches to a foot, then every piece of timber may be cut on the ground and ready for fixing.

To have a correct model of this roof let the drawing be on card-board, and cut in the following manner: Take C D as radius, also centres; draw arcs of circles at H and N; now take B as centre, and C as radius; intersect the arcs; join B H C and B N D; make a similar construction to this on line L E. The whole covering of roof being spread out, cut clear through all the outer lines; this done, make a slight cut on line L E and that of C D; also cut in a similar manner dotted lines B C and B D, and in like manner cut the covering which hinges on line L E. Now lift the piece and fold covering from you, bring the half hips together, and a perfect model of the roof is shown.

Plate 30.

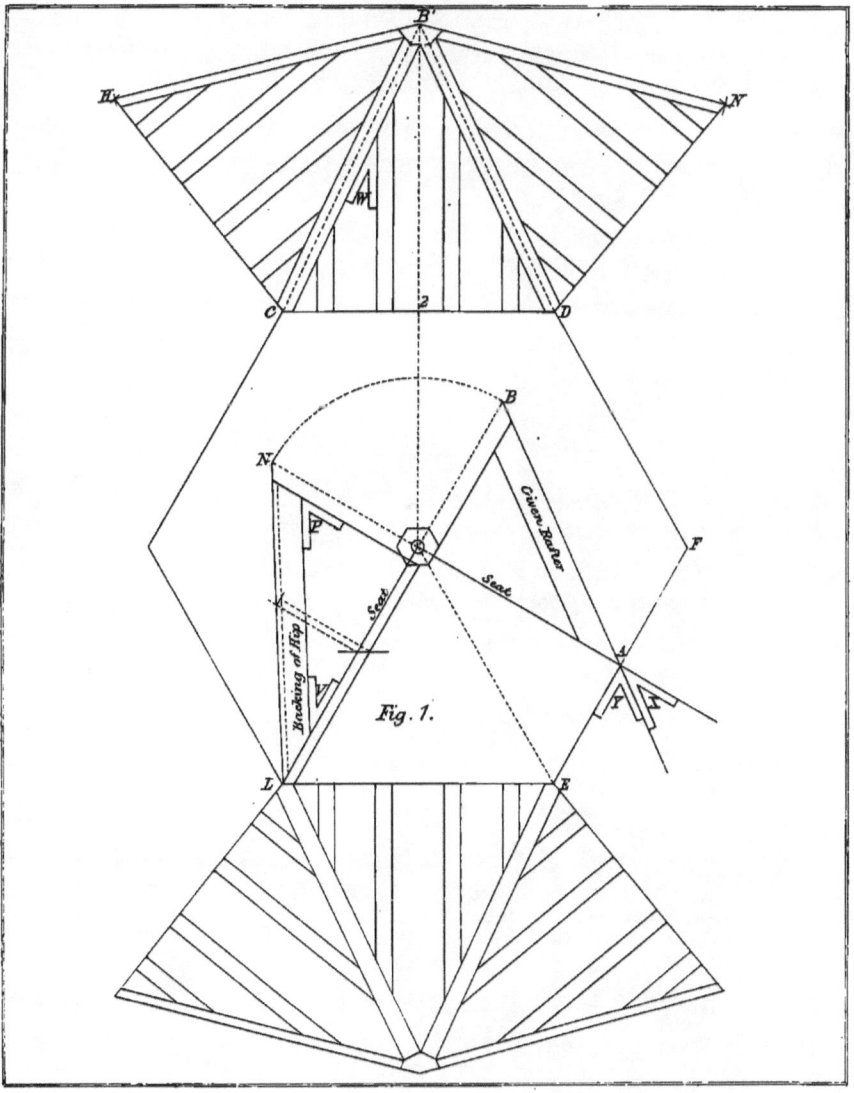

Fig. 1.

Plate 31.

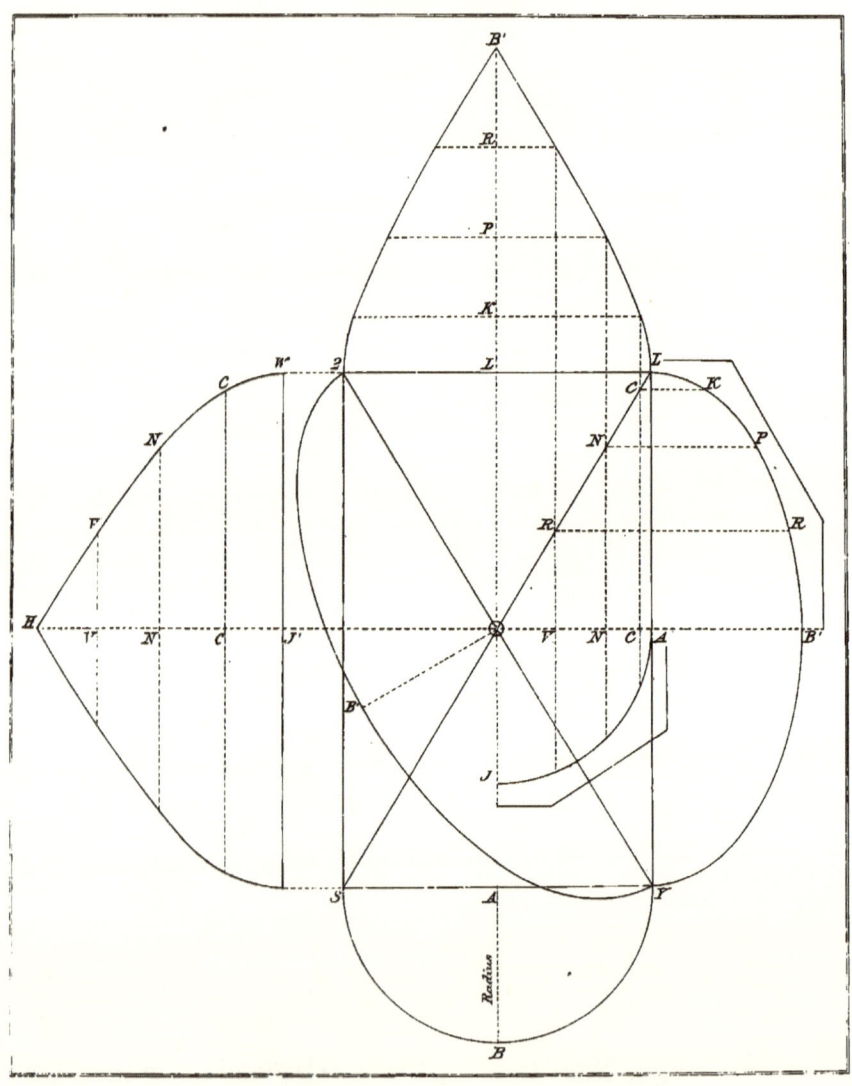

PLATE 31.

TO FIND THE RIBS AND COVERING OF A GROIN.

LET S 2 L Y be the ground-plan. Draw diagonals from corner to corner, intersecting in O; this done, draw on line S Y a semicircle, its radius being A B, which determines height of groin; draw through O, to the right and left, square with S 2; again draw through O parallel with S 2; take O as centre and A as radius; draw quarter circle A J; make A B equal A O; draw semi-ellipse L B Y; now draw from O square with diagonal 2 Y; make O B equal O A; this done, draw semi-ellipse 2 B Y. The ribs of groin are now in position. To find the covering, divide quadrant A J into any number of equal parts, say four; draw from each point parallel with Y L, cutting diagonal S L at R N C, from which draw square with Y L, cutting ellipse at K P R. These are measurements on the curve; set off the same above line 2 L L. In this way L K equals L K on curve, and K P equals K P on curve; again P R B equals corresponding letters on curve, thus giving points, through which draw parallel with 2 L, cutting lines from quadrant A J, and through intersections thus made draw the curve from B to L; set off distances on the left to equal those on right, and draw the curve from B to 2, which completes the end covering.

To find the covering of side S 2, take any point, say J; set off from it four parts, each to equal one of those on quadrant A J; draw through each point parallel with S 2; make C C equal C C on the right; again make N N equal N N on the right; once more make V V equal V R on the right; now draw the curve from H through V N C W; set off

distances on the other side, and draw a similar curve to that just made, which completes the side covering.

To have a correct idea of this, suppose the curved lines cut through the paper, and a cut made in like manner on line passing through J. Now the piece is loose, lift it, and bring edge through J on line S 2; bend the paper until point H stands over centre of groin O. Here the bending, has caused curved edges of covering to range with the straight lines O 2 and O S. Then if the end covering is cut in a similar manner, and bends from line 2 L L until point B stands over centre O, then its curved edges will be found to range with lines O 2 on the left and O L on the right, so that when the curved edges on both pieces of covering come together, they close directly over line O 2.

This problem and its solution should be well understood by metal-plate workers and masons.

We now come to the ribs. These are formed by a carpenter.

The view which this groin presents on looking through its narrow ends, is that of a semicircle, as shown on line S Y. Then it follows that all ribs which come in angle O L Y, must be parts of quadrant A J.

Again, the view presented on looking through the main arch is a semi-ellipse, as that of L B Y, parts of which are to be cut for angle O L 2. Then all the short ribs being cut to their proper lengths, and nailed to diagonal ribs, the groin is formed and ready for lathing.

PLATE 32.

CONSTRUCTION OF A ROOF HAVING HIPS AND VALLEYS.

THE ground-plan of this roof shows an extension on one front of the building, which occasions the necessity of having valleys.

Here it may be stated, that the usual rule of laying down a roof of this construction, is not only complicated, but obscure, owing to the multiplicity of lines and other details, making it almost impossible to understand their intention or meaning. But to obviate every difficulty in any construction, and to make all its parts perfectly clear, have the drawing on card-board, and cut in such manner as to fold, and show a correct model of the work, as is the object here.

We now commence by spreading out the covering of this roof, and show exactly "lengths and cuts" of every rafter. To obtain this, draw from angle E through T, cutting at R, and join T B; now determine on rise of roof, say T S; join S R E; draw from C parallel with B T, cutting at 5. This done, draw from angle A parallel with B T, cutting at K; draw from it parallel with A H; make K 4 equal T S; join A 4.

Now find the foot and down cut of all the rafters, except those of extension from line C D. This is done by drawing from S parallel with T R; make R L equal R K; square up from L, cutting through P, and draw from R through P. This gives bevel 7 for down cut, and bevel 8 for foot cut of all the rafters.

To find the covering for end of building A H and its side H G. Make R V equal R P; join V H; now take A 4 as radius, and with same radius take A and H for centres; make intersections at Y; join it with A H. These lines, to be correct, must equal line H V.

We now want a covering spread out, so that when in its position it will cover A B T K. To do this, take H for centre, and with any radius draw the arc 2.2; with same radius and A centre, draw arc 2.2'; make both arcs measure equal; draw from A through 2'; then draw from Y parallel with A 2'; make the distance on line A 2' measure equal to that of A B. This done, draw parallel with Y A, and we have the covering.

Adopt the same process to cover the end F G, as shown.

The bevel 6 is the side cut for jack-rafters, the down cut having already been obtained by bevel 7.

We now want to spread out the covering for the extension B C D E.

Commence at 5, and draw from it parallel with C D; take E S on valley-rafter for radius; with same radius, and C centre intersect line from 5 at J, and from same centre intersect dotted line at W; join it with C D; also join C J. Again, take C as centre and B as radius; draw the arcs B 3 and 3 3'; make both arcs measure equal; this done, join C 3'; draw from W parallel with C 3'; then draw from 3' parallel with C W. This completes the covering, with the exception of piece from line W D, which is equal to that just done.

Set off the actual position of rafters; this being done, shows that bevel X, gives side cuts for rafters which stand on line C B, and bevel 5 gives side cuts for rafters in angle C W D.

Here it will be noticed, that the exact lengths of rafters, are obtained by setting off half thickness of hips, on each side of hip lines spread out.

Let the drawing be made to a scale, say one and a half inches to a foot. By this means everything is done on the ground.

Work according to the drawing, and every piece of timber cut, will answer the purpose intended.

This drawing is presumed to be on card-board. It will show the necessity of being correct by cutting clear through all the outer lines. This done, make a slight cut on line H G to form a hinge, and for the same purpose, make a slight cut through lines F 2, A Y, W D, and W C. Now lift the piece and fold the covering from you, bring the hips together, and form the valleys, and we have a perfect model of the roof, showing the most simple and practical method that can be devised, for the length and cut of every piece of timber in it. This I have practically tested, and I hope it will be the means of assisting others, in more thoroughly mastering their trades, and ultimately open to them the way to success.

Plate 32.

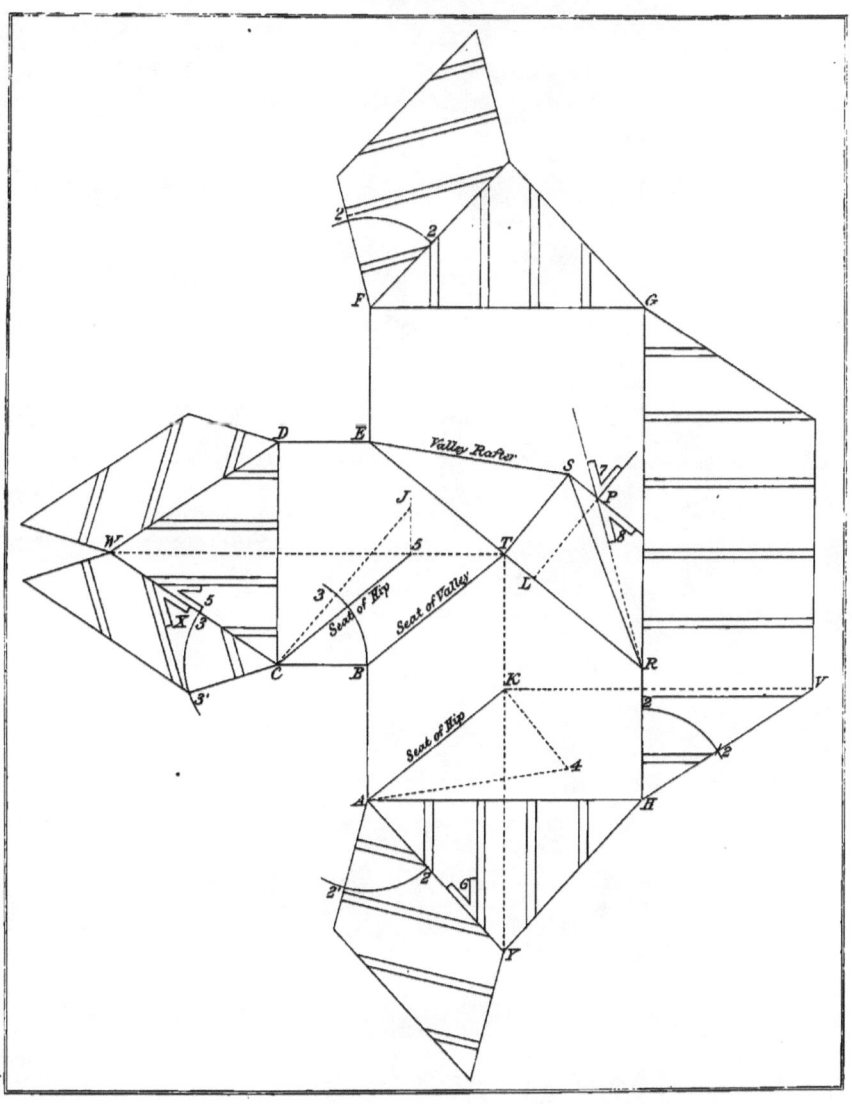

Plate 33.

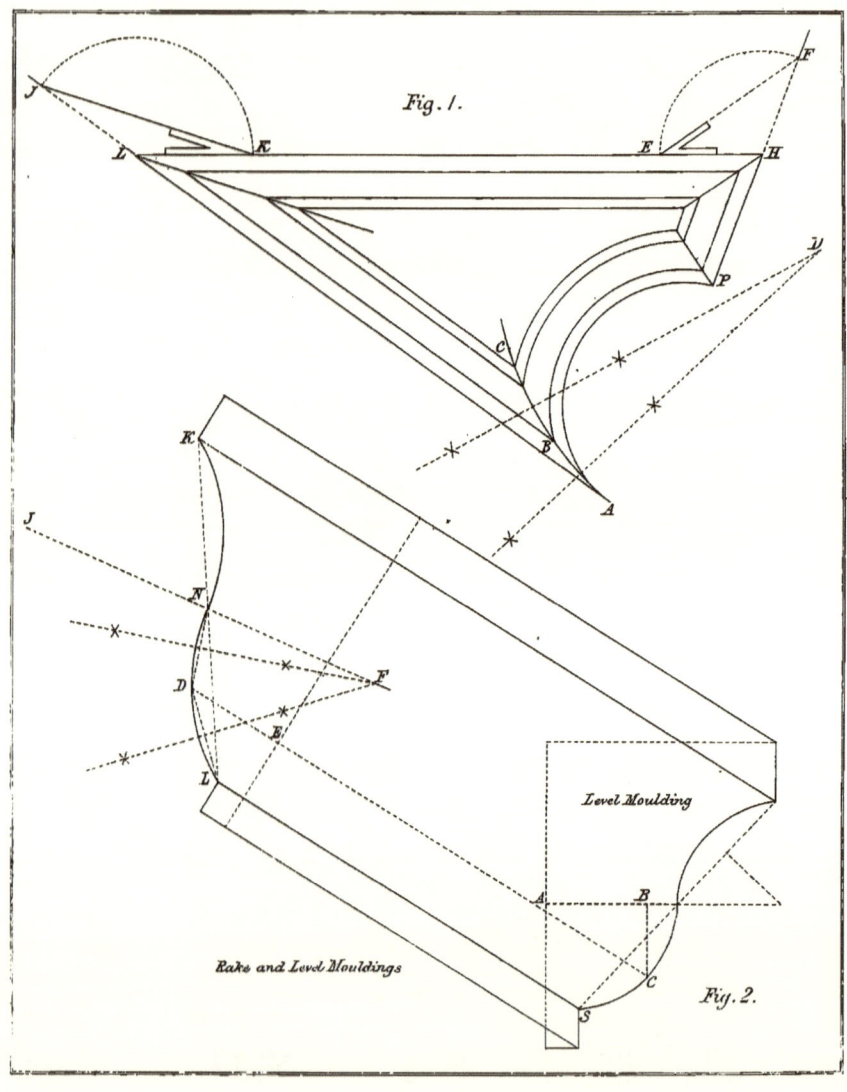

Fig. 1.

Fig. 2.

Level Moulding

Rake and Level Mouldings

PLATE 33.

THE INTERSECTIONS OF STRAIGHT AND CIRCULAR MOULDINGS.

FIGURE 1 shows the form of an irregular piece of framing or other work, which requires to have mouldings mitre and properly intersect.

The usual way of doing this is to bisect each angle, or to lay two pieces of moulding against the sides of framing, and mark along the edge of each piece, thus making an intersection or point, so that by drawing through it to the next point, which is the angle of framing, the direction of mitre is obtained. This process, however, is not the quickest and best by any means. The most simple and correct method is to extend the sides A L and P H.

Now suppose we wish to find a mitre from L; take it as centre, and with any radius, as K, draw the circle, cutting at J; join it and K; draw from L parallel with J K, and we have the mitre at once.

Now come to angle on the right; here take H as centre, and with any radius, as E, draw the circle, cutting at F; join it and E; draw from H parallel with E F, and you will find a correct mitre.

The next question is the intersection of straight and circular mouldings.

In the present case an extreme curve is given, in order to show the direction of mitre here, which is simply on the principle of finding a centre, for three points not on a straight line. For example, A B C are points; bisect A B and B C; draw through intersections thus made, and lines meeting in point D

give a centre, from which strike the circular mitre as shown.

Here it may be stated that in some cases a straight line for mitres will answer; this means when the curve is a quadrant or less.

Fig. 2 shows the intersections of rake and level mouldings for pediments.

The moulding on the rake, increases in width, and is entirely different from that on the level, yet both mitre, and intersect, the rake moulding being worked to suit the level. If the curves of Fig. 2, are struck from centres as shown, then by the same rule, the rake moulding is also struck from centres.

Take any point in the curve, as C; square up from it, cutting at B; draw from C parallel with S L; join L K, which bisect at N; make E D equal A B on the right; join L D and D N; bisect L D, also D N; draw through intersections thus made, and the lines meeting in F, give a point, from which draw through N; make N J equal N F; then F and J are centres, from which strike the curve, and it will be found to exactly intersect with that of Fig. 2.

Both mouldings here are shown as solid, and of the same thickness. This is done for the purpose of making the drawing more plain and easily understood; but bear in mind that all crown mouldings are generally sprung. This and mitreing will be fully explained in the next plate.

PLATE 34.

TO FIND THE FORM OF A SPRUNG OR SOLID MOULDING ON ANY RAKE WITHOUT THE USE OF EITHER
ORDINATES OR CENTRES.

It may not be generally known, that if a level moulding is cut to a mitre, that the extreme parts of mitre, when in a certain position, will instantly give the exact form of a rake moulding, and it will intersect, and mitre correctly with that of level moulding. To do this, take the level piece which has been mitred; lay its flat surface on the drawing; make its point P at Fig. 1, stand opposite point P at Fig. 2; keep the outer edge fair with line N L. The piece being in this position, take a marker, hold it plumb against the mitre, and in this way, prick off any number of points, as shown, through which trace the curve-line, and the result is a correct pattern by which the rake moulding is worked.

A moment's consideration, will convince us that this simple method, must give the exact form of any rake moulding, to intersect with one on the level.

To cut the mitres and dispense with the use of a box, this method will be found quick and off-hand. Take, for example, the back of level moulding, and square over on its top edge any line, as that of F N; continue it across the back to H; make H V equal T L above, and from V, square over lower edge H K. Now take bevel 2 from above, and apply it on top edge, as shown; mark F L; then join L V; cut through these lines from the back, and the mitre is complete.

To cut the mitre on the rake moulding, square over any line on its back, as that of H J; continue it across the top and lower edge; take bevel X, shown above Fig. 1, apply it here on top edge, and mark D A; take the same bevel, and apply it on small square at E, and mark E 2.

We now want the plumb cut on lower edge J K, and the same cut on front edge N P, shown at Fig. 2. Take bevel W above Fig. 1, apply it here and mark 2 B; join B A; this done, apply the same bevel on front edge N P, and mark the plumb cut, it being parallel with that of 2 B here, or K J, Fig. 2; now cut through lines on the back, and the mitre is complete.

102

Plate 34.

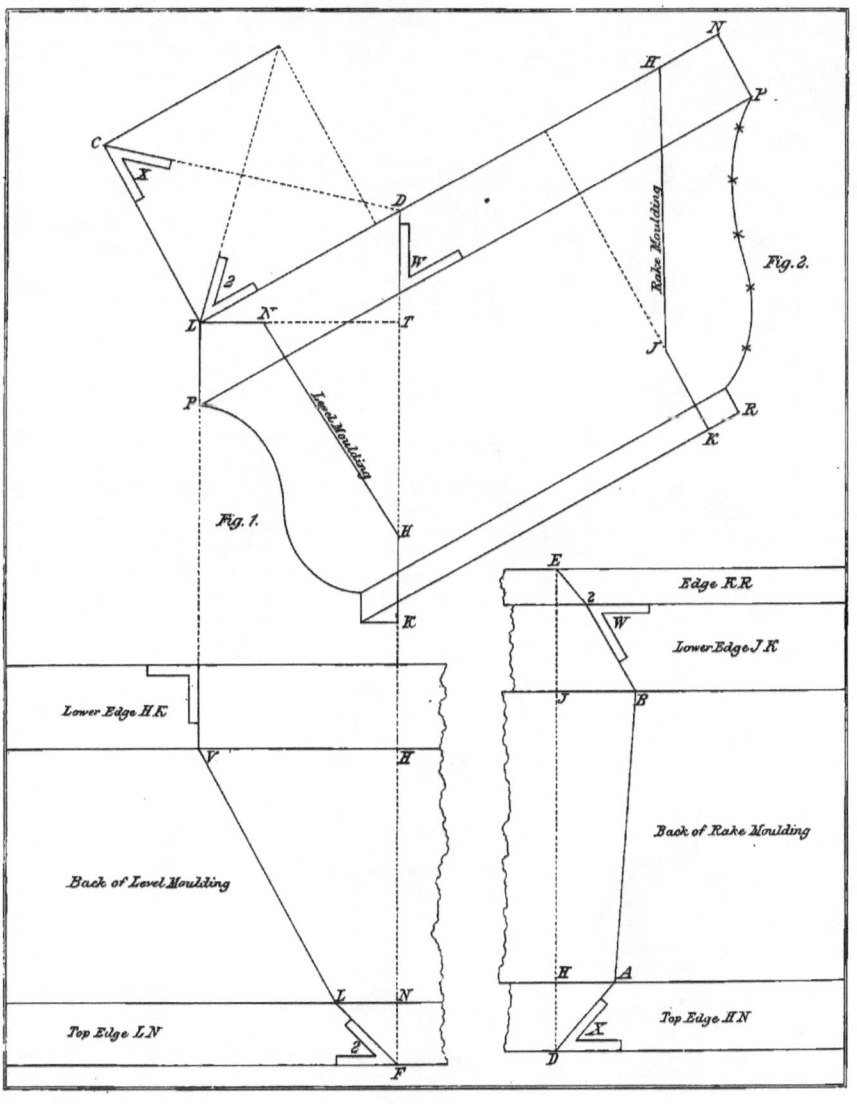

Fig. 2.

Rake Moulding

Level Moulding

Fig. 1.

Lower Edge H K

Back of Level Moulding

Top Edge L N

Edge R R

Lower Edge J K

Back of Rake Moulding

Top Edge H N

Plate 35.

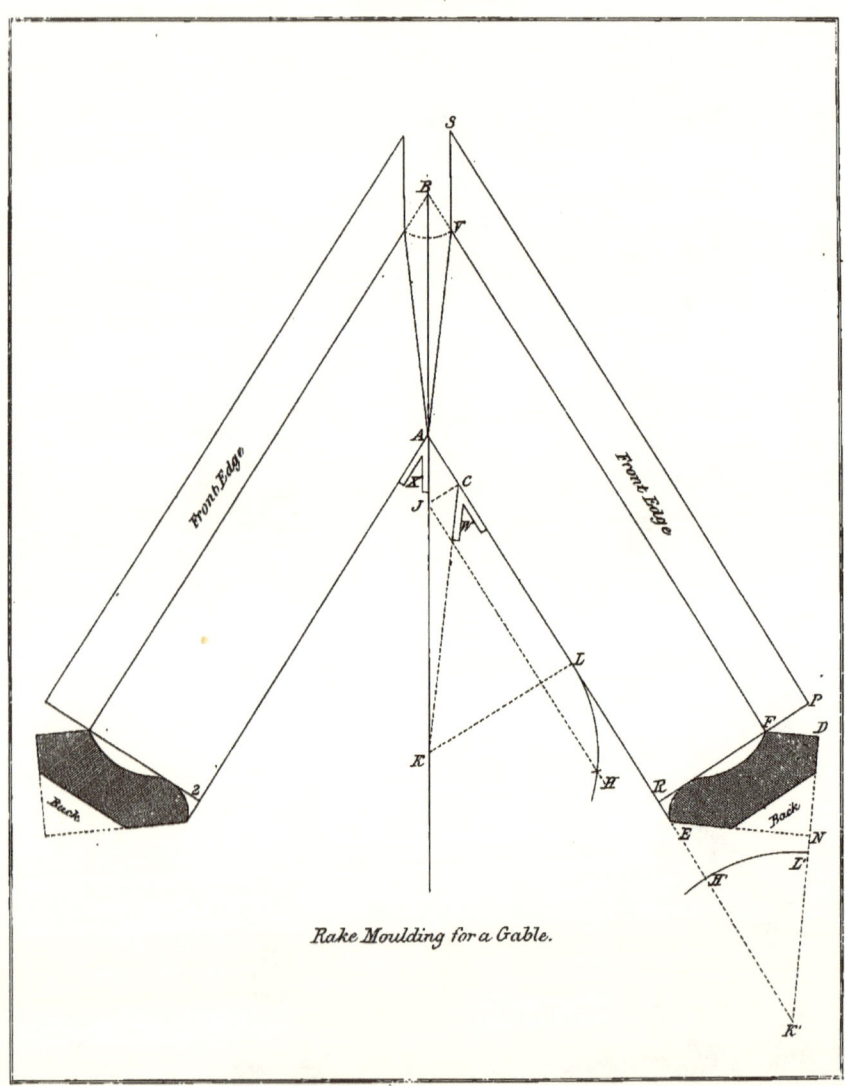

Rake Moulding for a Gable.

PLATE 35.

TO MITRE SPRUNG MOULDINGS ON A GABLE.

It has already been shown, that we dispense with making or using a box for mitreing sprung mouldings.

In this case, the front edge or upper member, stands parallel with face of wall, so that bevel X being applied, gives the plumb cut; then the cut on top edge is square with face of wall. This shows, that we have only to find the direction of a cut on the back of moulding to make the mitre.

To do this, take any point as R; draw from it square with rake of gable. Now mark sections of moulding, as shown, its back parallel with R F; draw from D square with E N; extend the rake to cut line from D at K; this done, take any point on the rake, say L; draw from it parallel with R F, cutting at K; take it as centre and L as radius, and draw the arc of a circle; with same radius return to K' on the right; take it as centre, and draw the arc

L' H'; make the first arc equal it; then draw from H parallel with L C, cutting at J; draw from it square with rake, cutting at C, and join C K. This gives bevel W for cut on back of moulding.

A most perfect illustration of this may be had by having the drawing on card-board, and cutting it clear through all the outer lines, including that of the moulding on lines F D N E, making a hinge by a slight cut on line R F; also make a hinge of line R A, by a slight cut on the back, and in like manner make front edge work on a hinge by a slight cut on line F V. This cut is made on *top* surface. Perform the same operation on the left. All the cuts being made, raise both sides on hinges A R and A 2; push the sections of mouldings on right and left from you; make front edge rest on F D. Now bring mitres together, and we have a practical illustration of mitreing sprung mouldings on the rake.

PLATE 36.

TO CONSTRUCT SPLAYED WORK, THE GROUND-PLAN FORMING EITHER RIGHT, ACUTE, OR OBTUSE ANGLES.

THE problem which is here presented, is one of more than ordinary importance, for by it is found, every conceivable cut that is requisite for framing, panelling, and boxes with slanting sides, or anything where angles are thrown out of square. In a word, it is immaterial how the angles of base are situated.

Our meaning of this will be, perhaps better understood by referring to Fig. 1. Here is given a "base" line as A D, on which is to stand slanting sides at any angle, say C B; the perpendicular height of work is D E. This shows that edges of sides are to be worked to bevel Z.

We will now assume a ground-plan, on which stand the slanting sides just given.

For this, come to Fig. 2. Here let T 2.3 S be the plan; set off width of sides to equal C B, Fig. 1. These are shown to intersect at P L above; then draw from P L through 2.3; these lines have intersected at C; take it as centre and A as radius; draw the semicircle A A, and with same radius come to Fig. 1. Take C as centre and draw the arc A B; take it in the dividers and return to Fig. 2. Here set off arcs A B on right and left, to equal A B, Fig. 1; draw through B on the right parallel with S 3, cutting at J and F; square over F H and J K, and join H C; this gives bevel X, as the cut for face of sides which come together at angle 3. The mitres

on edges of stuff are parallel with line L 3. The reason why this mitre is correct, is because the edges are worked to bevel Z, Fig. 1.

Now come to square corner at S. Here join K V; this gives bevel Y, for cut on face of sides which come together at square corners.

To find a bevel to cut the sides for angle 2. Draw from B on the left, square with A A, cutting at E; square over from it, cutting at N; join N C; this gives bevel W for cut on face of sides. The mitres on edges are found by drawing parallel with P 2. All the cuts and everything requisite for the work are now complete. It is understood that in actual practice, there is no necessity for spreading out the sides as here shown. The base of work and slant of sides being given, that alone is sufficient; but as we are particularly anxious that this construction should be clear and intelligible, let the drawing be on cardboard; then, by cutting through all the outer lines, including mitres, the piece becomes loose.

Now make a slight cut on the back opposite lines T 2.3 S. These form hinges for sides to work on. Again, make a slight cut on top surface along lines, which represent thickness of bevelled edges. Now raise the sides, bring the cuts together, and let the edges fall level; bring their mitres together, and we have a model of the work, its accuracy proved by its sides standing on given slant C B, Fig. 1.

Plate 36.

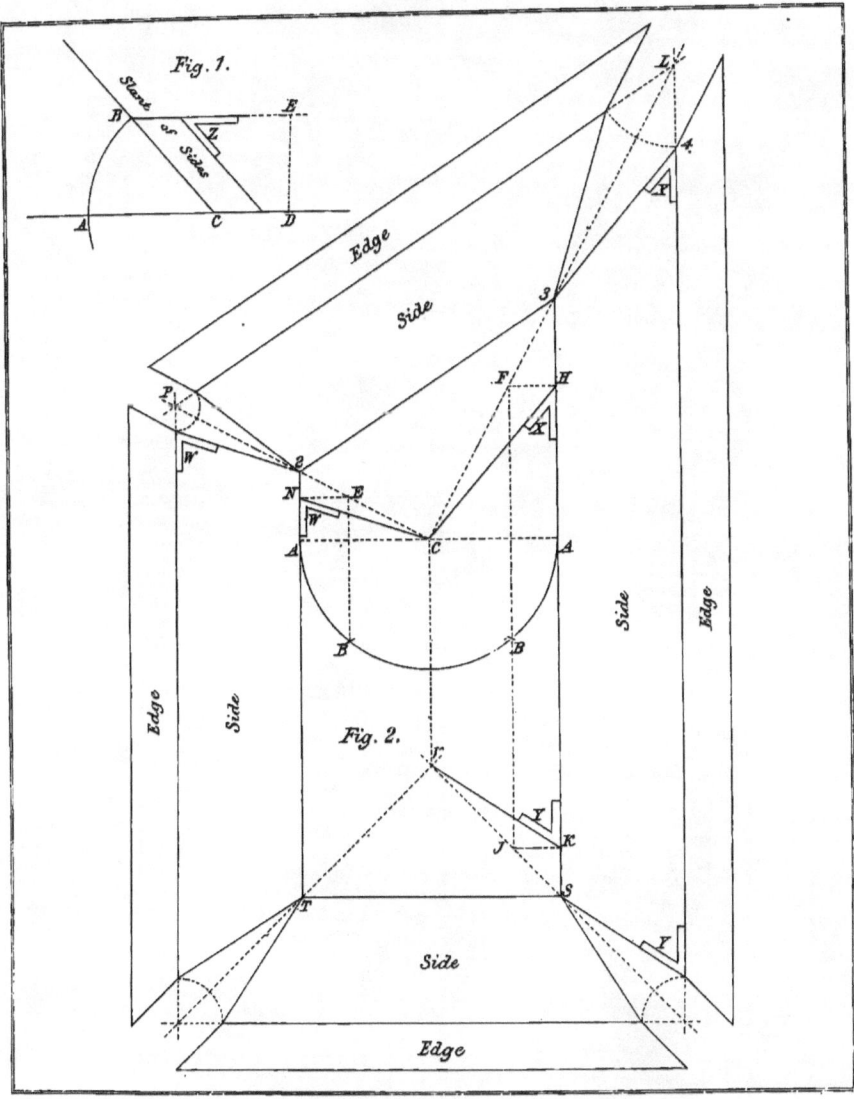

Fig. 1.

Fig. 2.

Plate 37.

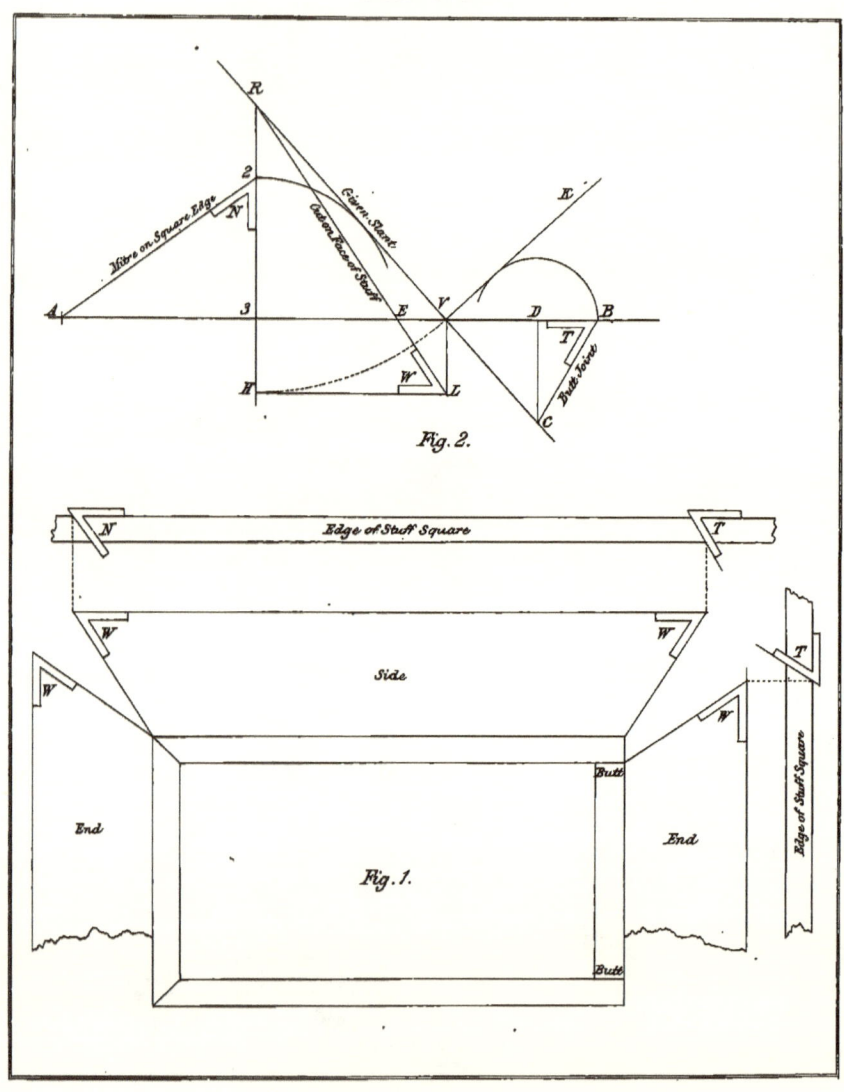

Fig. 2.

Fig. 1.

PLATE 37.

TO FIND BEVELS FOR CUTS ON SHOULDERS, AND FACE OF IRREGULAR FRAMING, OR ANY WORK WHICH INCLINES.

IN the preceding plate was shown that by first working the edges of inclined sides to a bevel, then the intersection of angle on the base, gives the mitre from V; draw from H parallel with 3 V, cutting at on edge of sides. But in this case the edges are to be square, which will make it necessary to find by construction a bevel for the mitre.

The following method, will be found quite simple for making either mitres or butt-joints, for any work which stands on a slant, the angles of ground-plan being square.

Fig. 1 is the ground-plan, or base of work, which is to have sides, each to stand on a given slant, and on the right the edges are to make butt-joints, and on the left to mitre. We leave this and come to

Fig. 2. Here draw a line, as A B, for a base; take any point on it, say V; draw through it a line on any slant desired, as V R. Again take any point on line A B, say 3; draw through it square with A B, cutting at R; make R H equal R V; square down from V; draw from H parallel with 3 V, cutting at L; join it and R. This gives bevel W, for cuts on face of sides and ends as shown on plan.

We now want a bevel for mitres on edge of sides and end, on left of plan. This is found by making 3 A equal 3 V. Take 3 as centre, and for radius a circle touching R V, cutting at 2; join it and A. This gives bevel N for the mitre.

The next question is a bevel for butt-joints. This is easily found by drawing V K square with V R; take any point as D; square down from it, cutting at C.

Now take D as centre, and for radius a circle touching V K, cutting at B; join it and C. This gives bevel T, to apply on edges of sides and end for butt-joints, as shown on plan, Fig. 1.

PLATE 38.

TO CONSTRUCT CYLINDERS, FORM RAMPS, AND CUT MITRE-CAPS.

WORKMEN differ in different cities as to the best and quickest methods of constructing cylinders. Some prefer bending a veneer over a form, which undoubtedly is a neat and clean method, the grain of wood running in the same direction as rake of stairs, thus giving to the work a perfect finish.

This method should always be adopted when the strings are hard wood; but if they are pine, or other wood which is to be painted, then we might dispense with making forms, bending veneers and backing the same, and instead have cylinders in staves. These should be well seasoned, the joints properly glued, and screwed from the back. It is known that cylinders done in this way have stood for more than a century, without showing a single joint. Then the only question to decide is, which of the two methods is the quickest and best. The workman may exercise his own judgment on this point — we leave it to him.

Fig. 1 shows a cylinder in three staves; each should be worked sufficiently long to make two or more cylinders; work the joints by bevel K; the piece being cut to proper lengths, let the square ends stand on the plan; see that joints are correct by the three staves forming the semicircle; bore for screws; put the cylinder together; prove its diameter, as being equal to that of plan.

Now take the pieces apart, glue the joints, and screw from the back.

Nails should never be used for fastening, and for this reason: the nail makes a bruise or burr on the surface of edge, and breaks the joint, or prevents it from coming together.

Fig. 2 shows the elevation of stairs at the starting. The centre of newel and position of mitre-cap are also shown.

The form of mitre which appears best, is to make L P equal half width of rail.

The mitre on the cap is made by means of having two saw-cuts in a block.

To find the distance that these cuts should be apart, draw from N centre of cap parallel with P A; this gives a distance as 2 A.

Now have a piece of plank, shown at Fig. 3; run a gauge-line on both sides, as that of A B; make A 2 and A C equal 2 A, Fig. 2, and square over the lines on end. Now take a panel saw, and make a cut through 2 and C, keeping thickness of saw towards A; this done, bring centre of cap on line A B; fasten with a screw; enter the saw at 2, cut one side of mitre down to 3; set the compasses to width of rail, and mark point C; this done, revolve the cap, until point C stands opposite cut C in the block; enter the saw and finish the mitre. If this is done properly, all fitting is avoided. In case a hole is made entirely through the cap for pin of newel, then bore for a pin in the block, and let the cap revolve on it instead of a screw.

Plate 38.

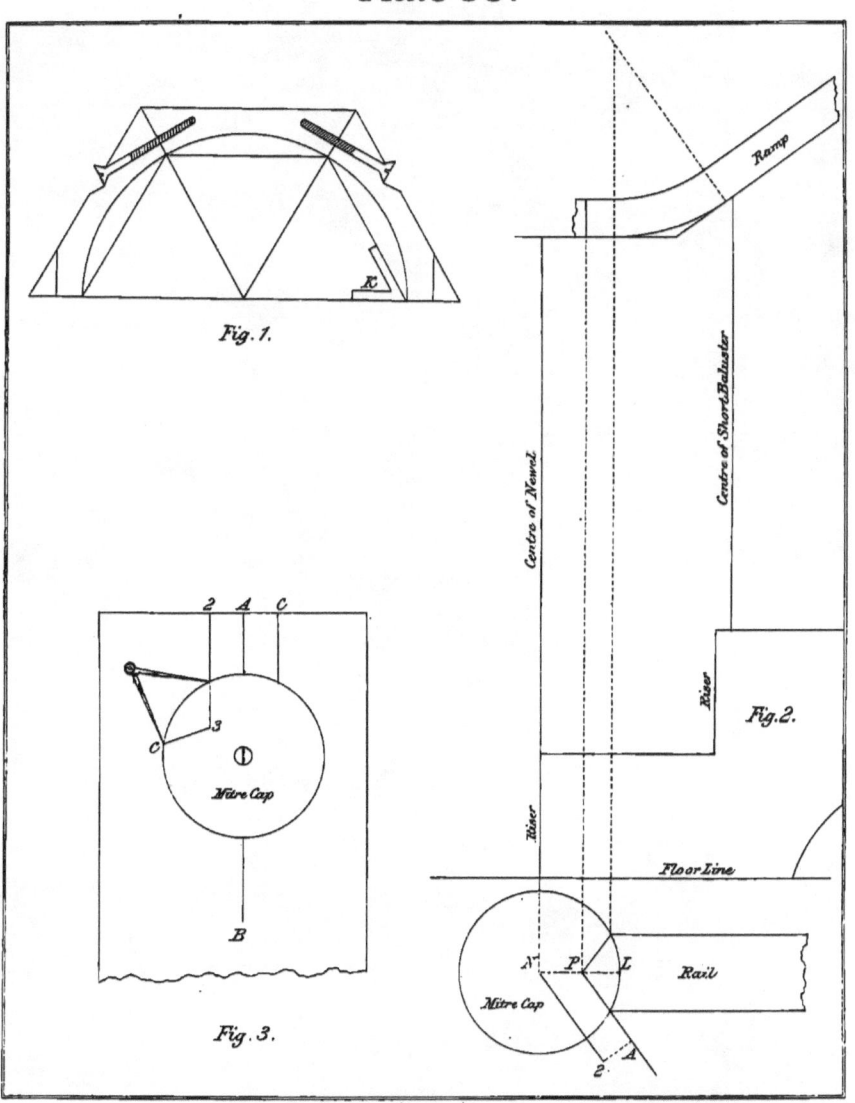

Fig. 1.

Fig. 2.

Fig. 3.

Ramp

Centre of Short Baluster

Centre of Newel

Riser

Riser

Floor Line

Mitre Cap

Rail

Mitre Cap

Plate 39.

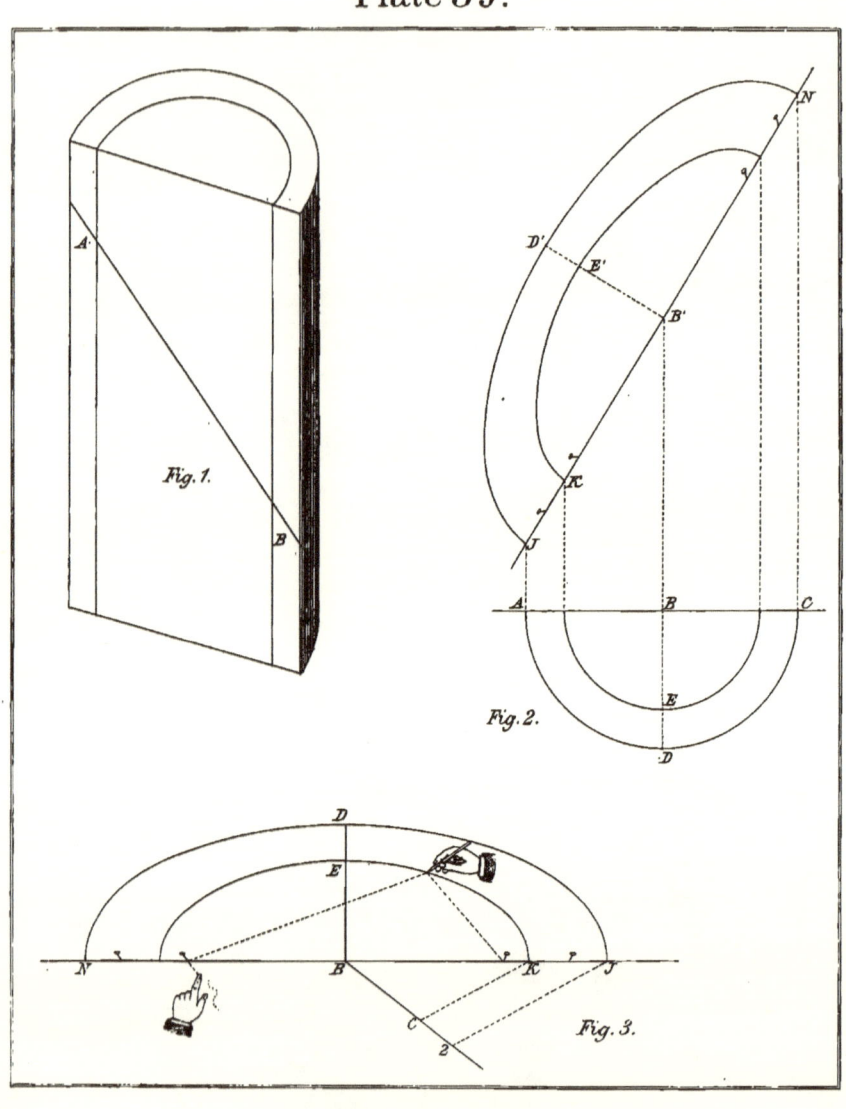

Fig. 1.

Fig. 2.

Fig. 3.

PLATE 39.

THE SECTIONS OF CYLINDERS.

FIGURE 1 shows a hollow semi-cylinder. If this is cut on any inclination as A B, the section of such cut must be a semi-ellipse. The feature which this section presents on its upper and lower ends, is that the width increases or diminishes according to inclination of cut; but on the short diameter the width never changes: it is always the same as thickness of cylinder.

These points should be understood by those who desire to acquire a knowledge of "hand-rail" construction.

To have a further illustration of this, come to Fig. 2. Here let A C be the diameter, and E D the thickness of a cylinder at its base. We will now draw a line, say N J, as the direction of a cut through the cylinder. This line is long diameter; square up the thickness, cutting at N above and J K below; square over B′ E′ D′. This line is the short diameter, and it is just equal to B E D at the base.

Here we see that the thickness of cylinder on short diameter is exactly equal to that on the base. It never changes: no matter how or on what the inclination of cut through the cylinder may be, the width remains the same.

The elevation conveys a correct idea of the semi-cylinder and its section; but for practical purposes it may be dispensed with. The short and long diameters being given are sufficient.

This will appear clear by referring to Fig. 3. Here the long diameter is given as N J, and the short as B E D.

To find the width of wide end at J, draw from B at any angle; make B C 2 equal B E D; join 2 J; draw from C parallel with 2 J, cutting at K; now find points for pins, and strike the curves with a string.

It is here evident that this semi-ellipse is just equal to the section of cylinder at Fig. 2.

PLATE 40.

LESSONS ON HAND-RAIL CONSTRUCTION.

MANY years ago I recommended the cutting of blocks as a means of instruction in this branch of joinery. At the same time 'I discovered the important system of bevels for butt-joints. This remains unchanged, unalterable, and ever must, because it is perfect. But nearly everything else has been thrown aside for newer and better ideas, and perfection at last attained. No more changes or alterations in this branch will be entertained or thought of. *It is now, for the first and last time, presented in a new light, clear, simple, and intelligible.* All ordinates are dispensed with — the angle of tangents found at once by drawing a single line. This alone has been the cause of our changing all previous thoughts and views on a matter which has been worn threadbare in more than a hundred publications on the subject.

The first problem being on card-board, and cut in such a manner as to convey the whole principle on which hand-railing depends. Examine it; the lines are few and simple, and yet it is the key by which any wreath can be produced.

Fig. 1 shows a square and quarter circle. Let us suppose this to be a ground-plan, over which is to stand a piece of plank or board, inclined to any angle, and we are required to cut it so that two of its sides shall stand exactly over two sides of the square, each edge of the plank making two unequal pitches, and in addition to this we must draw on its surface a curved line which shall range with every part of the quarter circle. Here it is evident that these conditions include everything that can be known about hand-railing, and to comply with them the two unequal pitches of the plank must be given. Then the first step is, extend K N on the right and left, likewise the sides 8 N and P K. Now assume K J as height for one pitch, also make K C equal K J; draw from J through C, cutting at D; make K A equal K N; join O A; the two pitches are now given, as D C and C A; these, when drawn on surface of plank, form a certain angle, the sides of which make tangents to an elliptic curve.

This angle is found by drawing from K square with J C; take C as centre and A radius; draw the circle, cutting line from K at E; join it and C; this gives D C E as the angle, which, being cut and placed in position over the square, shows the surface of plank making two unequal pitches, and angle D C F stands directly over two sides of the square, as K N and K P.

To find a curve on surface of plank that will range with quarter circle of plan. To do this, find the long and short diameters of a semi-ellipse by drawing from J through P; draw from 8 and N parallel with P J; again draw through 8, square with P J, cutting at 2 F; now square up from L, cutting at S; draw from D parallel with C E; make D R equal C E; join R S — this is short diameter: draw through R, square with R S, and we have long diameter. To find half its length, make N B on the right equal 2 F (through corner of square):

join B D; make N H equal N K; square up from H, cutting at R; this gives R D as half the long diameter, which transfer to Fig. 2, where corresponding letters are seen; make R V equal K N. Now find points for pins, and sweep the curve with a string; observe this curve just touches at E and D, thus making sides of angle D C E tangents to a portion of the semi-ellipse. The card being already cut, lift the piece and fold the pitches from you; bring the edges J K and C K together; let C E rest on pitch J P. Here is a practical solution of a simple yet important problem. Examine carefully the means which produce this result; endeavor to understand it thoroughly. This being done, lay the card in its original position, in order that we go a step further, by drawing a mould to suit the two pitches, and at the same time give bevels for butt-joints.

To do this, set a bevel or rule exact to angle E C D; now lift the rule and lay it on a piece of board, shown at Fig. 3; mark the angle E C D; draw from E parallel with C D; make E L equal C D; this done, come to Fig. 1 and take P 2 as radius; return with it to E as centre, and draw the arc; now draw through L, touching the arc, and we have the long diameter of a semi-ellipse. The short diameter is given by squaring up from L; make L O equal P 3, Fig. 1; set off on each side of O half width of rail; draw the joint at E; square with E C. The width of mould at both joints is obtained by having the bevels. To find these, take any convenient place, as Fig. 4; here draw two lines, any distance apart, but parallel with long diameter; take any point on lower line, say V; square up from it, cutting at R; this done, come to elevation above Fig. 1 on the right; here take D as centre, and with any radius draw the arc O O'; return with it to Fig. 4, and with V as centre draw the arc O O'; make both arcs measure equal, then draw through V and O, cutting at L; draw L N parallel with E C on mould; again draw L H parallel with E L, also on mould; take R as centre, and for radius a circle touching L N, cutting at T; draw from it through V — this gives bevel W for joint E; again take R as centre, and for radius a circle touching L H, cutting at K; draw through it and V — this gives bevel X for joint on the right. Both bevels being obtained, set off half width of rail below V, and draw parallel with V O' — this gives P V as half width of mould on each side of E the joint, and S V to set off on each side of N on the right. This done, come to Fig. 3, and make L R on long diameter equal R D at elevation above on the right; take F V at Fig. 4 and set it off on each side of R, and we have width of curves on long diameter, from which, and width of rail on short diameter, points are found for pins; by means of these we sweep the curves with a string, which completes the mould.

This is the first problem on hand-railing, and a most important one; for if it is clearly understood, there will not be the least difficulty in having a clear perception of all that follows.

Plate 40.

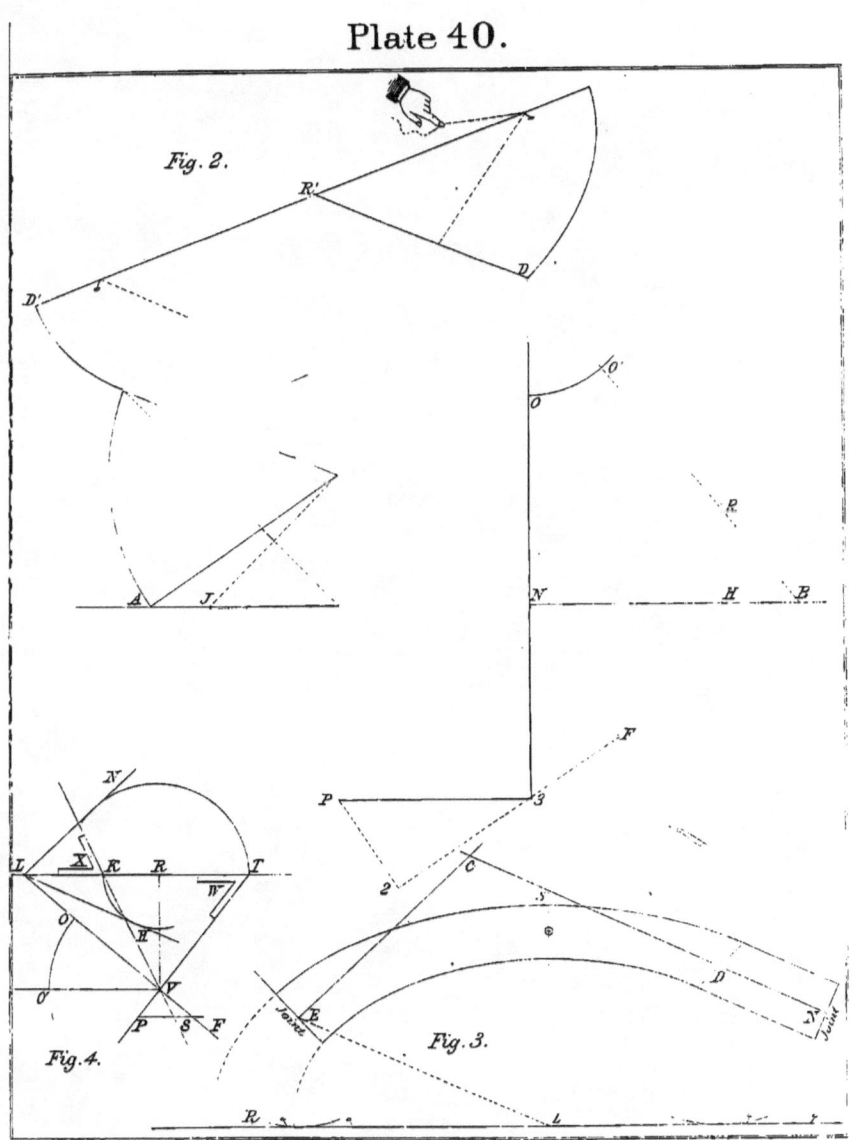

Fig. 2.

Fig. 4.

Fig. 3.

Plate 41.

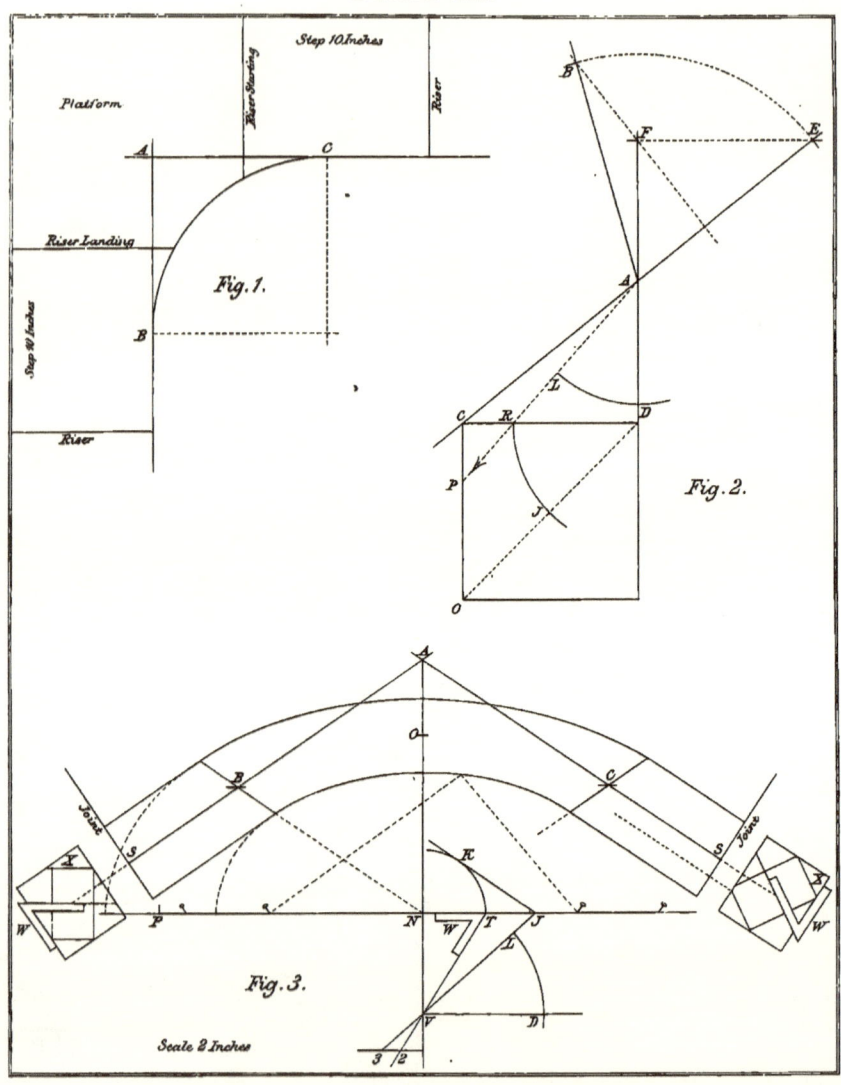

Platform

Step 10 Inches

Riser Starting

Riser

A   C

Riser Landing

Fig.1.

Step 10 Inches

B

Riser

B

F   E

A

L

C   R   D

P

J

Fig.2.

O

A

O

B   C

Joint

S   S   Joint

X   X

W   E   W   T   J   P   P   W

N   L

V   D

Fig.3.

Scale 2 Inches

3 /2

PLATE 41.

LESSONS ON HAND-RAIL CONSTRUCTION.

THE system of lines, as given and explained on preceding plate, will be adopted and applied throughout. Its teachings are simple, perfect, and reliable for the construction of every form of wreath, regardless of plan or situation of stairs. Its first practical application is to a simple wreath for quarter-landing stairs.

Fig. 1 shows the ground-plan. Two sides of the square are tangents to a quarter circle, which is the centre line of rail. Let us now place the risers on the plan, in such a position as will throw straight wood of wreath on the same pitch as the stairs. To do this, set off from A, half a step on each side of the square; now draw riser landing, and riser starting; set off from these the square steps, as shown. Any alteration of risers from the position given, would cause the wreath to be in two pieces, which in some cases is not objectionable; but here we have fixed the risers for a plain and simple wreath to be in one piece. In view of this, we will now make all clear and distinct in the following manner: At Fig. 2 (which is a square just equal to Fig. 1), extend the side from D; now place the pitch board on upper side of square, and draw from C through A; make A F equal A D; square over from F, cutting the pitch at E; draw through F; square with A E; take A as centre and E radius; draw the circle, cutting line through F at B; join it and A. This gives B A C as angle of tangents for the mould. Set a bevel or rule to it: this being done, lift the rule and lay it on a piece of board, shown at Fig. 3; now mark B A C; extend the lines to right and left; draw through B parallel with A C; make B N equal A C; draw from A through N—this line is the short diameter of a semi-ellipse, and to be correct, A N must equal O D; shown on square above; draw through N, square with N A, and we have long diameter; make N O equal O C on square above; set off on each side of O half width of rail.

The width of mould on straight parts is obtained by having a bevel for joints. To find this bevel, also half the long diameter of a semi-ellipse. Take any point, below N, say V; draw from it to the right; square with V N; come to Fig. 2; here divide O D in J; make D R equal D J; draw from A through R, cutting at P—this gives A P as half the semi-ellipse on long diameter (this line is also pitch of plank); take A as centre, and with any radius draw the arc L D; return with it to Fig. 3; here take V as centre, and draw arc L D; make both arcs measure equal; draw through V and L, cutting at J; draw J K parallel with C A on mould; take N as centre, and for radius a circle touching J K, cutting at T; draw from it through V—this gives bevel W to apply on both joints; make N P equal A P, Fig. 2; set off half width of rail below V, and draw it parallel with V D—this gives 2 V, as half width of mould on each side of S S at the joints; then 3 V being set off on each side of P, gives width of curves. The width of curves being thus given on long diameter, and width of rail on short diameter, directs the way by which we find points for plan, in order to strike the mould with a string, as shown. Make the joints square with S B and S C.

[Here it may be mentioned that plank for wreaths is required to be as thick as the rail is wide]: in other words, if a rail is four inches wide, have plank for wreaths four inches thick. Now let us cut the stuff square through; then face one surface of the piece out of wind; this being done, lay the mould on; mark the joints by it, and at the same time mark on surface of plank, the direction of tangents, which are on the surface of mould; by means of this, joints may be proved as to their being correct or otherwise; have a nine or twelve inch square, which is perfectly true, and apply it, by bringing the stock against the joint; see that edge of blade, and surface of plank agree; and for the other application, keep the stock against the joint; see that blade of square, and line on surface of plank agree. Here remember, that joints are the most important matter in hand-railing, for if they are not correct, it will be impossible to make the rail stand over its plan; no attempt at forcing the rail to its position will answer, because there is a liability of breaking the joints, and rendering the work useless. [Keep these facts in mind.]

Now proceed, and give the wreath piece its cylinder form, by drawing the tangents across the joints, and square with surface of plank; also square over both edges opposite line through O; this done, mark half thickness of stuff on each joint, and on edges opposite O. Now take bevel W, and apply it to the joints; mark square sections of rail as shown; then cut off slab X on the left from top side, and slab X on the right from under side; work by the bevel, and at the same time have the edges square with joints; this being done, square over half thickness of rail, continue it along bevelled edges, and square with joints; set off on this line the distance S B, and through the extreme point draw the spring line by the pitch board; the line made by bevel W on square section being continued on surface of plank, and the mould having tangents, as S B and S C, on both sides, lay it on the piece, keep its outer edge flush with bevelled edge, and inner edge fair with dotted line on the right. Now tangents on the mould are directly opposite lines on surface of plank—one end of mould projects past the joint, as is always the case in every application. Mark along the edges; this done, apply the mould in like manner to the under side. Now take off the slabs, and in doing so, hold the plane in the same direction as spring lines on bevelled edges; this being done, we are ready to bring the piece to a thickness, which is quite simple, because the square section of rail is marked on each joint, and the thickness on both edges opposite short diameter through O; here the slabs are equal, and when taken off, the wreath piece is found to be of a parallel width throughout. This could not be the case had the mould been prepared in a careless and slovenly manner, as is too often done, followed by cutting, filing, and tinkering to get the thing look like a wreath. Avoid this by starting aright, and working true to every line. Remember that "Jack of all trades and master of none" is a homely maxim, but true. Learn to do one thing well; it matters little what it is, only do it well, and you need never have fears as to success.

In regard to the application of moulds for giving wreath pieces their cylinder form, there is only one correct way, and that is, keep tangents on the surface of mould opposite tangents on the surface of plank. This is the whole secret in a few words. Here understand that it is the bevels for joints, which direct the tangents on surface of plank.

PLATE 42.

LESSONS ON HAND-RAIL CONSTRUCTION.

FIGURE 1 shows the ground-plan for a side wreath, starting from a newel; the wreath to form its own easing from the mitre-cap; its straight wood thrown on the same pitch as that made by a square step and riser; the newel to project from straight string any distance desired; two or more ends of steps at the starting are curved. To do this, proceed as follows:

Fig. 2 is the elevation of a square step and riser; the centre of short balusters indicated by 2 E, on which rests the under side of rail. Here the height of newel is determined as being equal to the length of a short baluster and one riser added: this means from top of first step to under side of mitre-cap. Now assume 2.3 as length of tangents for ground-plan; make B 3 on the left equal 2.8, (here observe that B is the centre of a baluster standing in the same position as that of 2 on the right;) draw from B any angle to suit projection of newel, say B N; make B N equal B 3; draw from N square with N B; now draw from 3 square with 3 B, cutting line from N at P, thus making P a centre, from which is drawn the curve on ground-plan. Set off from N sufficient wood for mitre; this done, lay the pitch-board on B 3, and draw pitch B C.

To find angle of tangents for the mould, draw from N square with B 3, cutting at T; draw from it square with B C; take B as centre and N radius; draw the circle, cutting line from T at A; join it and B; this gives A B C as the angle. Before leaving here, find half the long diameter of a semi-ellipse, in order that curves on mould may be drawn by means of a string. To do this, draw from B square with B N; draw from 3 parallel with B N, cutting at J; make 3 K equal B J; draw from C through K; make 3 H equal 3 P radius; square down from H, cutting at V. This gives V C as half the long diameter; the same line is also pitch of plank on its surface along the square edge. Now set a rule to angle A B C; this done, lift the rule and lay it on a piece of board, shown at Fig. 3; mark A B C; extend B C, say to J; draw through it square with J C; set off from A sufficient wood for mitre, or to equal that shown on ground-plan; work the joint square with A B; this being done, lay the piece down, bring a straight edge against the joint, fasten both, lay down a strip of same thickness, and draw on it the line through A square with A B; this done, make A V equal V C, Fig. 1; square up from V; make V 3 equal radius P 3; set off half

width of rail on each side of 3. The width of mould is obtained by having the bevels for joints. To find these bevels, draw a line at any distance below the long diameter, but parallel with it; say the line is that of S L on the right, take any point on this as L; square up from it, cutting at N; now come to upper part of plate at C; take it as centre, and with any radius draw arc D S; return with same radius to L as centre; draw the arc D S; make both arcs measure equal; draw through L D, cutting at E; draw E F parallel with B C on mould; take N as centre and for radius a circle touching E F, cutting at H; draw from it through L. This gives bevel Y for joint on straight part of wreath: its application is shown on square section above. The line L E having already given bevel W, its application is shown on square section to the left.

To find width of mould at both joints, set off below L half width of rail, which draw parallel with S L; this gives K L to set off on each side of J, at joint on mould, and F L to set off on each side of A to the left. Now find points for pins, and sweep the curves with a string, which completes the mould.

The plank having been cut square through, and joints made, apply bevels W and Y; mark square sections of rail, as shown; this done, take off the slab on outer edge of straight part, and from top surface, work it by bevel Y, and at the same time have bevelled edge square with joint; this done, apply a square, and mark half thickness of rail; continue this along bevelled edge and square with joint; then set off on line just made the distance C J, and at its extreme end mark the plumb-line by the pitch-board. Now lay the mould on, keep its outer edge flush with bevelled edge of stuff, and its joint at wide end even with joint of stuff, making line A B on mould stand opposite line on joint made by bevel W; mark surface of plank as edges of mould direct; apply the mould in like manner to the under side. Now take off the slabs, and in doing this, hold the plane in the same direction as plumb-line on bevelled edge. The wreath piece having its cylinder form, cut off under slab of straight part and under slab at joint A; here mark the mitre, and cut it, but not entirely through until the moulding is done. Now work off the remainder of slab as concave corner directs, forming the best possible easing; gauge to a thickness, and we have a perfect side wreath.

Plate 42.

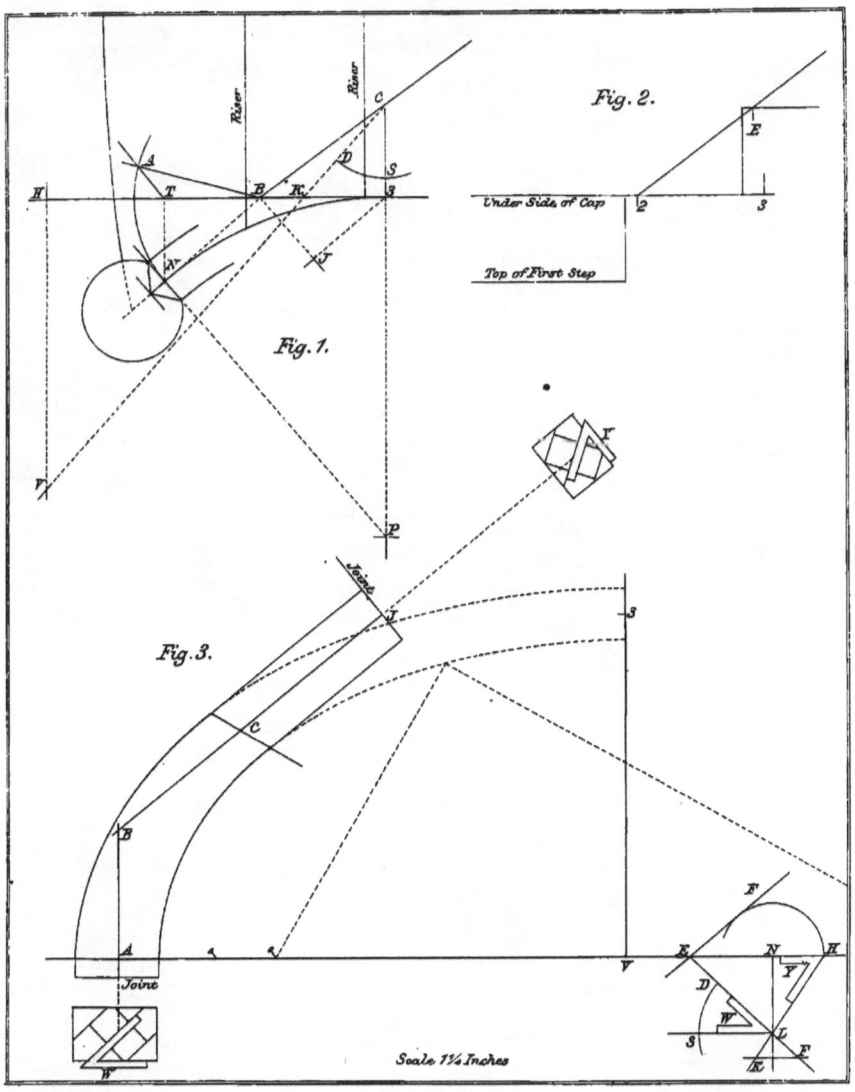

Riser

Riser

Fig. 2.

Under Side of Cap

Top of First Step

Fig. 1.

Fig. 3.

Joint

Joint

Scale 1¼ Inches

Plate 43.

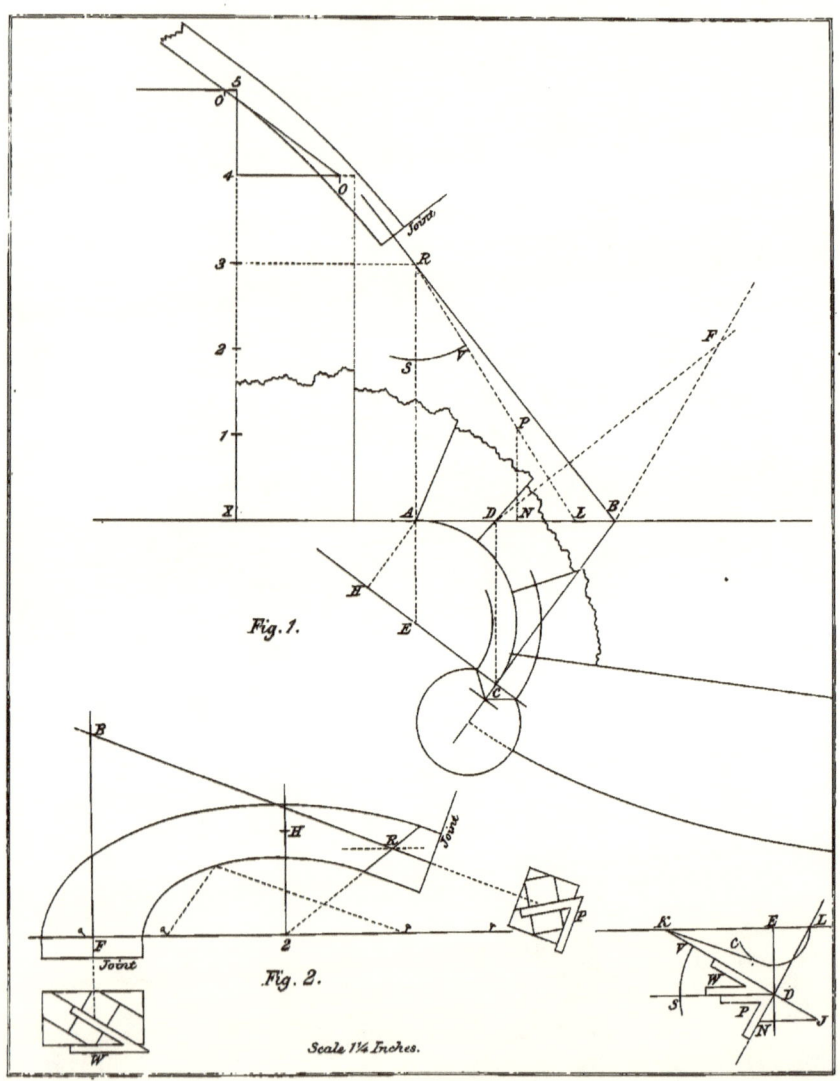

Fig.1.

Fig. 2.

Scale 1¼ Inches.

PLATE 43.

LESSONS ON HAND-RAIL CONSTRUCTION.

FIGURE 1 shows a ground-plan for the starting of stairs. The curve given for centre line of rail is greater than a quarter circle. Here understand that the radius is not limited; it may be less or more, to suit the passage or situation of stairs, and still have any number of winders required. But remember, that to have the curve for centre line of rail just a quarter circle, and no more, that alone would make it impossible, to give a proper easing to lower part of wreath, starting from the mitre-cap, which is the very place most conspicuous in the stairs, and where no defects of any kind should be seen, nor need there be, if a little judgment is exercised in laying down a plan similar to that which is here given. The point E, being the centre from which the curve is drawn for centre line of rail, take any point on it, as C; draw from C through E; again draw C B square with C E. This makes tangents A B C, which are of equal length. Now set off the number of winders required, say five, as shown; the ends on centre line of rail being equal to half a square step, have the first winder at the newel wider. Now determine height of newel from top of first winder to under side of mitre-cap, say it shall equal a short baluster, and one riser added. This understood, make an elevation by setting off from X five risers; this done, draw the square step, and let under side of rail rest on centres of short balusters O O; square over from 3, cutting line through E A at R; draw from B through R. This line is the pitch of one tangent on surface of plank. Now form a ramp; let half its thickness be on each side of line R B. This completes the elevation. To find angle of tangents for the mould, draw from C square with A B, cutting at D; draw from it square with B R; take B as centre and C radius; intersect line from D at F; join it and B. This gives F B R as the angle of tangents.

Let us now find half the long diameter of a semi-ellipse, in order to strike curves on mould by means of a string. To do this, draw from A, parallel with B C, cutting at H; make A L equal H C; join L R. This line is pitch of plank, as its square edge stands over C H on plan. Now make A N equal radius E C; square up from N, cutting at P. This gives P R for half the long diameter. We are now ready to set a rule to angle F B R. This done, lift the rule and lay it on a piece of board,

shown at Fig. 2; mark F B R; set off from F the wood for mitre to equal that on plan; draw the joint square with F B; set off from R a distance to equal that shown on elevation from joint of ramp to R; then make the joint square with R B. If the board is not sufficiently wide to draw long diameter on the surface, lay it down; bring a straight edge against the joint at F; fasten both; lay down a strip, and draw on it the long diameter square with F B; make F 2 equal P R at elevation above; square up from 2; make 2 H equal radius E C on plan; set off half width of rail on each side of H. To determine width of mould at both ends, we have to find bevels for joints. To do this, take any convenient place on the right; here draw two lines any distance apart, but parallel with long diameter; take any point on lower line as D; draw through it square with D S, cutting at E. This done, come to elevation above. Here take R as centre, and with any radius draw the arc S V; return with it to D as centre; draw the arc S V; make both arcs measure equal; draw through D and V, cutting K; draw K O parallel with R B on mould; take E as centre, and for radius a circle, touching C K, cutting at L; draw from it through D. This gives bevel P for joint at R, its application, shown on the joint by square section. The line D K, having given bevel W, and its application to the joint, is shown on the left. Now set off half width of rail below D; draw it parallel with D S. This gives J D to set off on each side of F at wide end of mould, and N D to set off on each side of tangent at R on mould. Now find points for pins, and sweep the curves with a string, which completes the mould. Let us examine it and see that everything is understood. First prove that F B R is the actual angle of tangents, this being a most important point. And to test it, draw any line for a base, as that of F 2; square up from F; make F B equal C B on plan. Now take the distance H A on plan, and set off the same distance above the base, indicated by dotted line through R. This done, come to elevation above; here take R B as radius; return with it to the mould; take B as centre, and intersect dotted line. Now observe that the intersection thus made has just cut point R, which shows in the clearest manner the accuracy of this new discovery in hand-railing.

PLATE 44.

LESSONS ON HAND-RAIL CONSTRUCTION—PLATFORM STAIRS.

FIGURE 1 is the ground-plan. The semicircle shows centre line of rail, its radius being six inches, the steps ten inches wide. To have the risers on plan in a position, that will cause both rail and string to present the best possible effect. This is done by placing one baluster on the platform opposite A, the position of baluster fixed, set off from it; the others on centre line of rail. The distance apart is five inches, or equal to half a step. This arrangement gives clear directions to draw riser E on the right, and riser D on left, set off from these the width of two steps, as shown, and draw riser landing and riser starting. The face of latter should be curved in order to bring nosing of step into the cylinder. This curve may be worked in the solid. We have now a plain statement of the manner in which the ground-plan for platform stairs should be laid down. And here let it be remembered that the same rule applies to stairs having cylinders, of six or fourteen inches in diameter; but beyond that, it is best to arrange the risers *so as to have three balusters on platform.* Let us now go to work and find a correct mould for this wreath, which is done by unfolding or spreading out four times the radius A B on a board, as shown at Fig. 2. Here lower margin of plate may be considered the edge of a board, from which are drawn dotted lines; these show four divisions, each being equal to radius A B of plan. Here it may be mentioned that all principal lines in hand-railing are right angles and parallels. The best and quickest way to draw them is by a framing square, it having a fence or stop, which is done by taking a strip, say two inches wide; make a cut through its edges at each end. This done, slip the piece on blades of square; fasten the ends with a screw. Here you have a tool with a fence to slide along the edge of drawing-board; and by means of it right angles or parallels are quickly made on any surface, as in the present case, where are shown steps and risers spread out and standing exactly in the same position as those on plan. This being understood, draw the pitches through corners of square steps on right and left, cutting through D and B. Join D B; square over E H and F W, which gives K as a point. Now find angle of tangents for the mould, by drawing from K square with B C; take B as centre and F radius; draw the circle, cutting line from K at A; join it and B. This gives A B C as the angle. Before leaving here let us find half the long diameter of a semi-ellipse, for the purpose of drawing curves on mould by means of a string. To do this, make K N equal K W; square over N R; extend pitch C B, cutting at L; draw

from it through N; draw from W parallel with L N; again draw through R; square with N L, cutting at P and T; make H J on the left equal P T; join J F. Then 2 F is half the long diameter of semi-ellipse. It is also pitch of plank. Now set a rule to angle A B C; this done, lift the rule and lay it on a piece of board, shown at Fig. 3; mark A B C; extend B C for straight wood; draw from C parallel with B A; make C 3 equal B A. Now come to Fig. 2; here take P N as radius; return with it to mould; take A as centre, and draw the arc of a circle at 2; then draw through 3, touching the arc at 2; and we have position of long diameter. This, observe, may be given independent of point 3; and in this way, take T W at Fig. 2 as radius; bring it to the mould; take C as centre, and draw the arc as shown; then a line touching both arcs produces long diameter. This understood, make 3.2 equal F 2 at Fig. 2; square up from 3; make 3 O equal A B on plan; set off half width of rail on each side of O. The width of mould at each end is obtained by having bevels for joints. To find these bevels, take any convenient place on the board as Fig. 4; here draw two lines any distance apart, but parallel with long diameter on mould; take any point on lower line, say 3; draw through it square with 3 V, cutting through L. This done, come to Fig. 2; here take F as centre, and with any radius draw the arc S V; return with it, and take 3 as centre; draw the arc S V; make both arcs equal; draw through 3 and S, cutting at A; draw A B parallel with A B on mould; again draw A C parallel with B C on mould. This done, take L as centre, and for radius a circle touching A B, cutting at R; draw from 3 through R. This gives bevel H for joint A. Its application to joint is shown by square section; then half width of rail being set off above L, and drawn to cut at P, which gives P R as half width of mould on each side of A at the joint. The bevel for joint on straight part of wreath is found by taking L as centre, and for radius a circle, touching A C, cutting at N; draw from it through 3. This gives bevel W for joint D. Its application to joint is shown by square section on the right; set off half width of rail below 3; draw it parallel with 3 V. This gives J 3 as half width of mould on each side of D at the joint; then K 3, being set off on each side of 2 on long diameter, gives width of curves. Now find points for pins, and sweep the curves with a string, which completes the mould. Remember, that when bolting the two pieces of wreath together, to keep the lines made by bevel H on each joint opposite.

Plate 44.

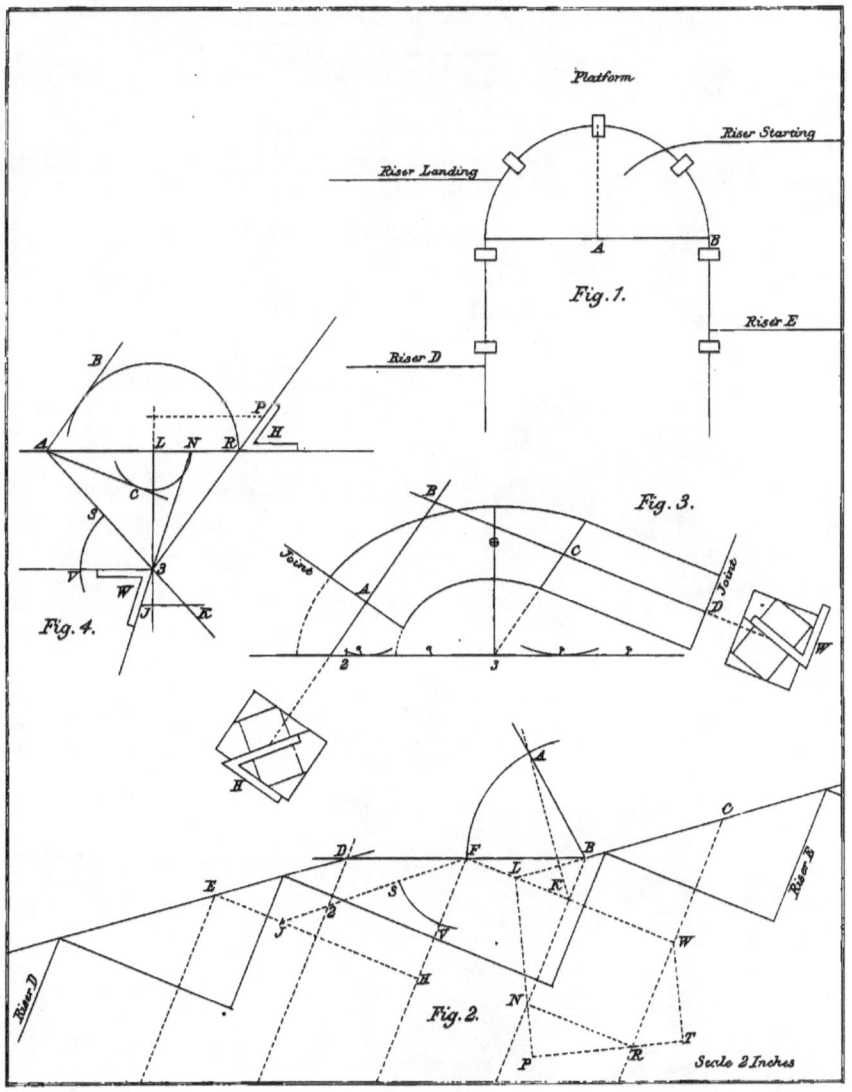

Platform

Riser Starting

Riser Landing

A

B

Riser E

Riser D

Fig. 1.

Fig. 3.

B

A

P

H

L   N   R

C

S

Joint

B

C

Joint

Joint

D

W

3

V

W

J

K

Fig. 4.

2

3

H

A

C

Riser E

D

F

L

B

E

S

K

2

V

J

W

H

N

Riser D

T

P

R

Fig. 2.

Scale 2 Inches

Plate 45.

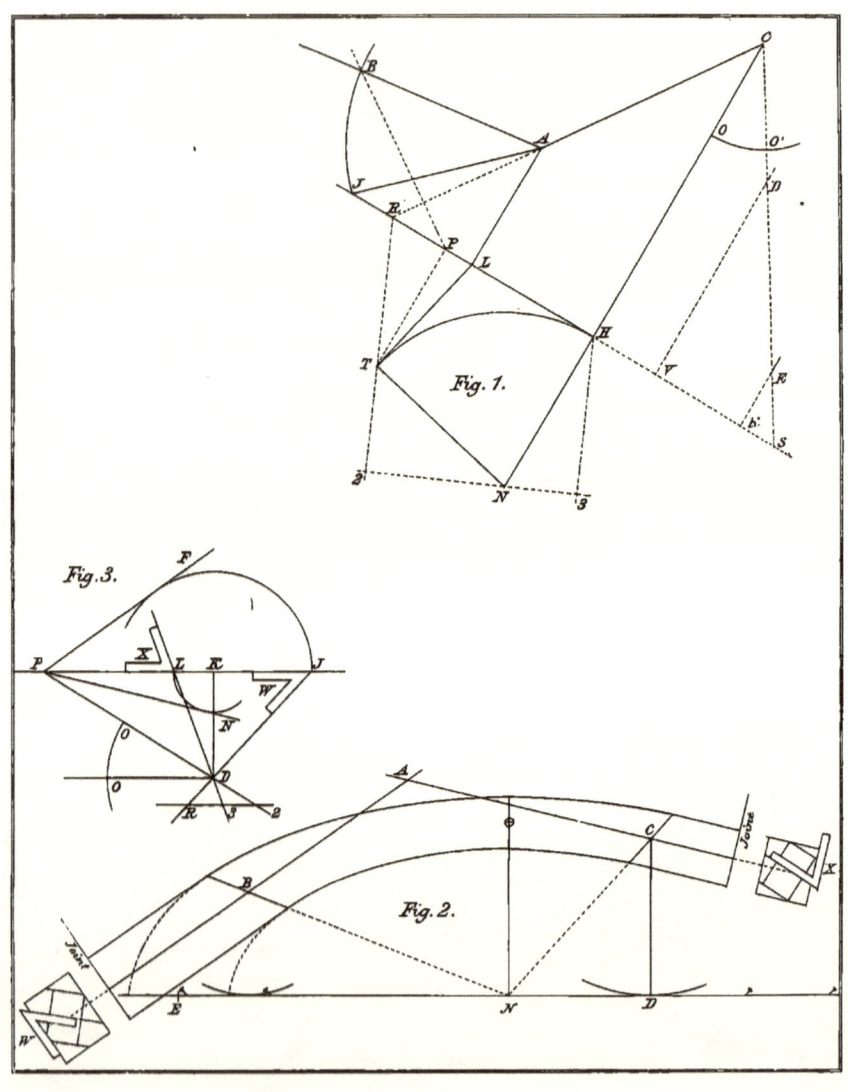

Fig. 1.

Fig. 3.

Fig. 2.

PLATE 45.

LESSONS ON HAND-RAIL CONSTRUCTION.

FIGURE 1. Here we change the ground-plan, which is less than a quarter circle, in order to show how easy this system adapts itself with equal certainty to every conceivable form of wreath, regardless of plan or situation of stairs. The present case fully illustrates this. Here we have to find a mould that will produce a wreath which has two unequal pitches, and is to stand correctly over its plan.

To solve this problem is not difficult. Let us commence by extending tangent L H to right and left, and in like manner extend line N H; this done, square up a line from L; assume the upper pitch as C A; extend it, cutting at R; now make L J equal L H; join A J. This is lower pitch: both pitches form a certain angle on surface of plank, that when in position, stands directly over tangents H L and L T.

To find this angle, draw from T square with L H, cutting at P; draw from it square with A C; take A as centre and J radius; draw the circle, cutting line from P at B; draw from A through B, and we have B A C as the angle for the mould.

We must now find half the long diameter of a semi-ellipse, in order to strike curves on mould by means of a string. To do this, draw from R through T; draw from H parallel with R T; now draw through N square with T R, cutting 2.3; make H S equal 2.3; join S C; make H K equal H N; square up from K, cutting at E; then E C is half long diameter of semi-ellipse.

To find position of short diameter on mould, make H V equal N 3; square up from V, cutting at D; this gives D C. Here understand that line S C is pitch of plank: this means on its surface and square edge when standing in position over line 2.3 on plan.

We are now ready to draw the mould. Set a bevel or rule to angle B A C; this done, lift the rule and lay it on a piece of board, shown at Fig. 2; mark B A C; extend these lines for straight wood, and make joints square with them; lay the piece down, and if not sufficiently wide to show long diameter, lay another piece alongside; fasten both; this done, come to Fig. 1; take 3 H as radius; return with same radius, and from C as centre draw the arc at D; come again to Fig. 1, and take 2 T as radius; return with it, and from B as centre make the arc as shown. Now draw a line touching both arcs, and we have long diameter; then draw from C square with diameter, cutting at D; make D N E equal E D C on the right of Fig. 1; this done, square up from N; make N O equal radius N H, Fig. 1; set off on each side of O half width of rail. The width of mould at each end is determined as usual by having bevels for joints. To obtain these bevels, take any convenient place on the board as Fig. 3. Here draw two lines any distance apart, but parallel with long diameter at Fig. 2; take any point on lower line, say D; square up from it, cutting at K; this done, come to upper corner of plate on right; here take C as centre, and with any radius draw the arc O O'; return with same radius to D, and with it as centre draw arc O O'; make both arcs equal; draw through D and O, cutting P; draw P F parallel with B A on mould; again draw P N parallel with A C on mould; take K as centre and for radius a circle touching P F, cutting at J; draw from it through D; this gives bevel W for joint at wide end of mould, as square section shows. Again take K as centre and for radius a circle touching P N, cutting at L; draw through it and D; this gives bevel X for joint at narrow end of mould, as shown by square section on the right.

To obtain half width of mould at each joint, and width of semi-ellipse on long diameter, set off below D half width of rail; draw it parallel with D O'; this gives 2 D to set off on each side of E, and R D as half width of mould on wide end; then 3 D is half width of mould at narrow end on the right. Now find points for pins, and sweep the curves with a string, which completes the mould.

PLATE 46.

LESSONS ON HAND-RAIL CONSTRUCTION.

FIGURE 1 shows a ground-plan where curve for centre line of wreath is greater than a quarter circle; this is just the reverse of that given on preceding plate. This wreath, like the last, is to have two unequal pitches. The rule already given holds good in this case as it will in every other, no matter what the character of wreath may be. The constructive principle is simply a repetition of practical truths; still, we may derive some advantage by looking over this plate, as it shows how the lines may be contracted into the least possible space, by means of which we dispense with great unwieldy drawing-boards, — a consideration of no small importance where room is limited.

Let us now proceed with the explanations. The curve for centre line of rail is struck from point N, and is inclosed by tangents meeting in L. Here it may be well to remember that any two tangents from a circle, as those of H L and T L, are always equal or the same length. But tangents to an elliptic curve may be unequal, and yet made to stand exactly over equal tangents to a circle, as will be the case here. To understand this point, extend L H to right and left, and in like manner extend line N H; square up a line from L. Now assume C A as upper pitch for wreath; square over A J; join J L. This is lower pitch; or we may make it the upper, and C A the lower. Proceed to find angle of tangents for an elliptic curve. To do this, draw from T square with L H, cutting at P; draw from it square with A C; take L J as radius; with same radius and A centre intersect line from P at B; join it and A; then we have B A C as the angle, which, being in position, will stand directly over T L and L H. And if an elliptic curve was drawn, it would range with circle of plan. But to make everything clear, find half the long diameter of a semi-ellipse and pitch of plank, in order that curves on mould may be drawn by means of a string. To do this, extend upper pitch C A, cutting at R; draw from it through T; draw from H parallel with T R; now draw through centre N square with T R, cutting 2.3; this done, make H S equal 2.3; join S C. This is pitch of plank. Make H K equal radius N H; square up from K, cutting at E. This gives E C as half long diameter of semi-ellipse. To

find position of short diameter, make H V equal 3 N; square up from V, cutting at D. This gives D C.

We are now ready to draw the mould in the usual way, by setting a rule to angle B A C; this done, lift the rule and lay it on a piece of board, shown at Fig. 2; mark B A C; extend the lines for straight wood, and make joints square with them; come to Fig. 1; here take 3 H as radius; return with it to C as centre; draw the arc at D; come again to Fig. 1; take 2 T as radius; return with it, and take B as centre; draw the arc as shown. Now draw a line touching both arcs, and we have position of long diameter; draw from C square with diameter, which gives point D; make D N equal D E on pitch (above Fig. 1 to the right); make D E equal D C (also on pitch); square up from E; make E O equal radius N H, Fig. 1; set off on each side of O half width of rail. The width of mould at each end is obtained by having bevels for joints.

To find the bevels. These may be given on a separate piece of board, or at any convenient place, as Fig. 3. Here draw two lines any distance apart, but parallel with long diameter. Take any point on lower line, say A; square up from it, cutting at K; this done, come to upper part of plate at C; take it as centre, and with any radius draw the arc O O'; return with same radius to point A, and with it as centre draw arc O O'; make both arcs measure equal; draw through A and O', cutting at P; draw P F parallel with A B on mould; take K as centre and for radius a circle touching P F, cutting at J; draw from it through A, and we have bevel W for joint at wide end of mould; square down from P, cutting at H; draw H L parallel with A C on mould; take P as centre and for radius a circle touching H L, cutting at Y; draw from it through H. This gives bevel X for joint at narrow end of mould on the right. Now set off half width of rail below line A H; draw it, cutting through bevel lines, which gives 2 A to set off on each side of N at Fig. 2; then 3 A is half width of mould at wide end, and R H is half width of mould on narrow end to the right; draw the straight wood parallel with tangents A B and A C. Now find points for pins, and sweep the curves with a string, and the mould is complete.

Plate 46.

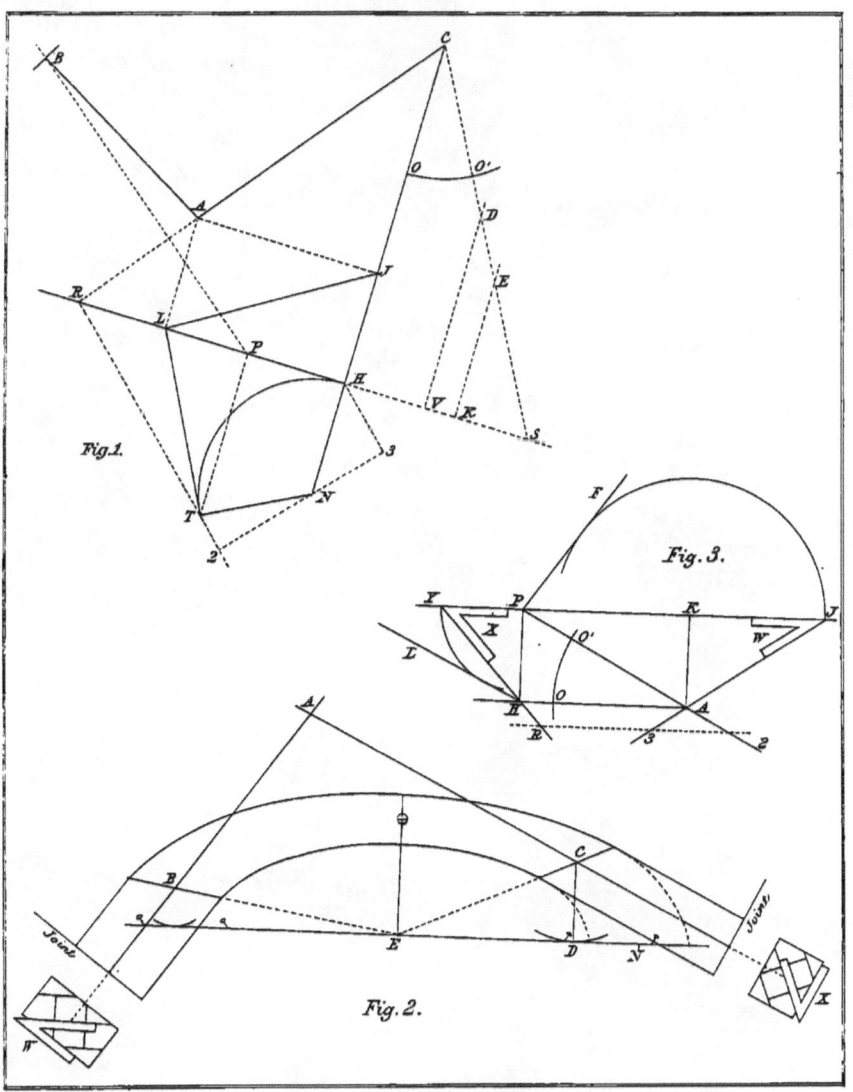

Fig.1.

Fig.3.

Fig.2.

Plate 47.

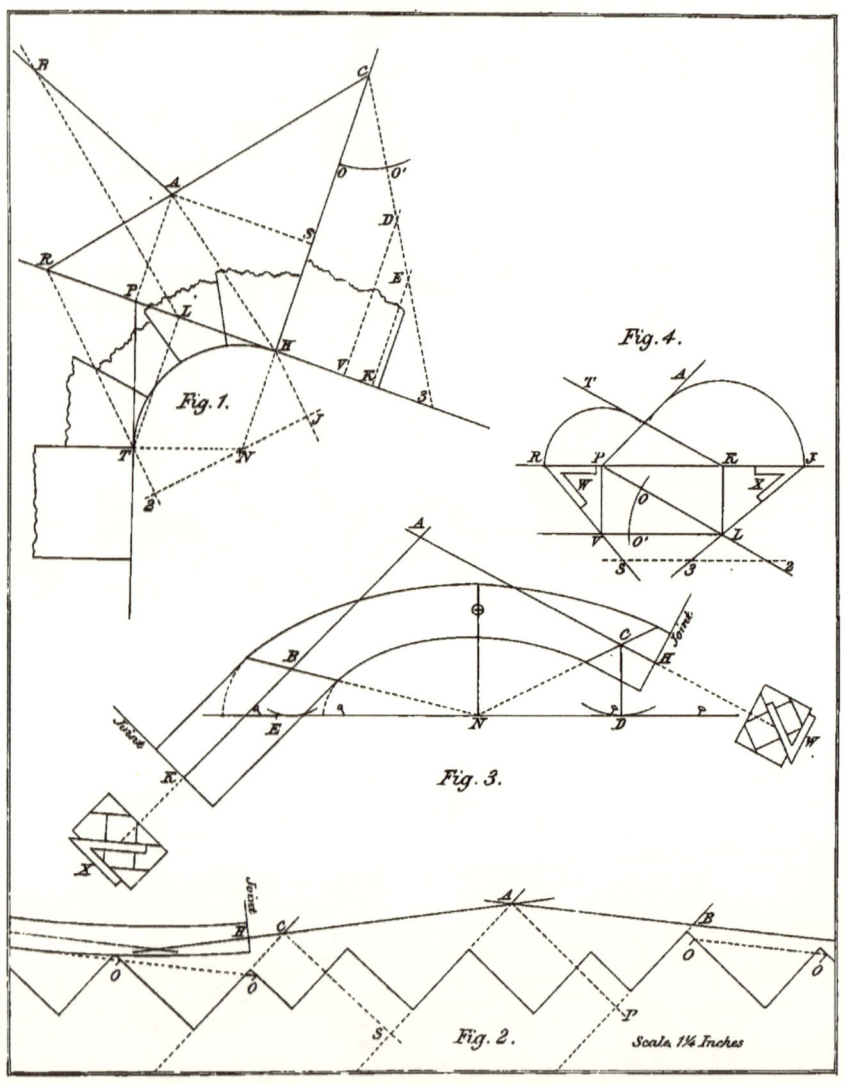

Fig.1.

Fig.4.

Fig.3.

Fig.2.

Scale, 1¼ Inches

PLATE 47.

LESSONS ON HAND-RAIL CONSTRUCTION.

This drawing gives a practical illustration of preceding plate. The explanations here, and in fact throughout, are necessarily repetitions, because the constructive principle is the same in every particular, and applies to all forms of wreath.

Fig. 1 shows the ground-plan of stairs having four winders in the circle, with square steps above and below; the tangents for centre line of rail form an acute angle and meet in point P. This wreath is to be in one piece; its upper end to form a ramp, and connect with straight rail over the square steps.

To do this, extend the tangent P H to right and left; draw from centre N through H; then square up a line from P. We now want the exact pitches for this wreath, which is soon given by spreading out the tangents P T and P H; also the winders and two square steps. This is shown at Fig. 2. Here they stand in precisely the same position as those of Fig. 1. The square steps on right and left show centres of short balusters, as O O. Let under side of rail rest on these; set off half its thickness, and draw the pitch, cutting through B A; then A is a fixed point, from which draw through C, or in such manner as to form an easy ramp; this done, draw from A square with risers, cutting at P, which gives P B as one height; now draw from C square with risers, cutting at S; this gives S A for lower height; transfer height P B to Fig. 1, and make P A equal it; square over A S; make S C equal S A, Fig. 2; draw from C through A, cutting at R; join A H; this being done, proceed and find angle of tangents for the mould, by drawing from T square with P H, cutting at L; draw from it square with A R; now take A as centre and H radius; intersect line from L at B; join it and A. This gives B A C as the angle: its sides are just equal to pitches B A C, Fig. 2. Before leaving here, find pitch of plank, and half the long diameter of a semi-ellipse, and position of short diameter. To do this, draw from R through T; draw from H parallel with T R; again draw through N square with T R, cutting at 2 J; make H 3 on right equal 2 J; join 3 C; now make H K equal radius H N; square up from K, cutting at E. This gives E C as half the long diameter of semi-ellipse.

To find position of short diameter, make H V equal N J; square up from V, cutting at D. This gives D C.

We are now ready for the mould. First set a bevel or rule to angle B A C; this done, lift the rule and lay it on a piece of board, shown at Fig. 3; here mark B A C; extend these lines for straight wood; make C H on right equal C H on the left at ramp below; draw through H square with C A; make straight wood B K on the left any length desired; draw through K square with B A; this done, come to Fig. 1, and take H J as radius; return with it to C as centre, and draw the arc as shown at D; come again to Fig. 1, and take 2 T as radius; return with it to B as centre; draw the arc shown at E; now draw a line touching both arcs, and we have position of long diameter. This done, draw from C square with diameter, cutting at D; make D N equal D C above Fig. 1 on the right; then make N E equal E C at same place above; now square up from N, and make N O equal radius N H, Fig. 1; set off on each side of O half width of rail.

The width of mould at each end is obtained by having the bevels for joints. To find these bevels, come to any convenient place on the board as Fig. 4; here draw two lines any distance apart, but parallel with long diameter at the mould; take any point on lower line, say L; square up from it, cutting at K; this done, come to upper part of the plate at C; take it as centre, and with any radius draw the arc O O'; return with it to L as centre; draw the arc O O'; make both arcs measure equal; then draw through L and O, cutting at P; draw P A parallel with A B on the mould; take K as centre, and for radius a circle touching P A, cutting at J; draw from it through L. This gives bevel X for joint at K on the mould. The square section shows the application of bevel X. Proceed and find a bevel for joint at H on the mould. To do this, draw K T parallel with C A on mould; square down from P, cutting at V; take P as centre, and for radius a circle touching T K, cutting at R; draw from it through V. This gives bevel W, its application to the joint shown by square section on the right. Now set off half width of rail below V L, indicated by dotted line. This gives S V to set off on each side of H on the mould, and 3 L to set off on each side of K, also on the mould; then 2 L being set off on each side E on long diameter, gives width of curves. By means of these and width of rail on short diameter, points are found for pins, which, being fixed, take a string, sweep the curves, and the mould is complete.

PLATE 48.

LESSONS ON HAND-RAIL CONSTRUCTION.

FIGURE 1. We now come to the last plate, where is shown a ground-plan, differing from any that has yet been given. Still, the same rules and system of lines are here applied as in every other case, so that this plate may be considered to exhaust the subject entirely. To add anything further would not only be useless, but cumber the work to no purpose. Nor is it necessary, as we are confident that the instructions already given, if followed, are quite sufficient for any intelligent workman to become a master of this branch of joinery.

Let us now proceed with the explanations. In the first place, enclose centre line of rail by tangents; this being done, draw riser landing; set off from it on tangent half a square step as A B; now set off from B on centre line of rail the number of winders required; let the spaces apart be equal to A B. The next question is to find the exact pitches for the wreath. To do this, unfold or spread out three times the radius N P on a narrow board, as shown at Fig. 2, and indicated by dotted lines from lower margin of plate, which may be considered the edge of a board; now set off the winders, and one square step to stand here in the same position as those on plan. The measurements are taken from points where risers cut tangents. This being done, we have the elevation of tangents, winders, and one square step as a guide to draw the pitches; then let under side of rake-rail rest on centre of short balusters O O, as shown on square step; set off half its thickness; now come to floor line on the left; here draw under side of rail to stand half a riser above the floor; set off half its thickness, cutting at D, it being a fixed point, from which draw, say through B, and from B draw through A, or in such manner as to give the ramp an easy curve at the junction of winders and square steps. Here it is seen that lower wreath piece is to have two unequal pitches. This is done for the purpose of making the rail more uniform in height over the winders, which would not be the case if a straight line had been drawn from D through A. The upper wreath piece forms its own ramp on the landing.

To find the heights of both pieces, draw from point A parallel with the steps, cutting at P. This gives P C as the lower height. Now draw from C square with C P, cutting at E. This gives E D for upper height. Let us now prepare for drawing the mould, by forming a square on that at Fig. 3, which is equal to one of those on plan. This done, extend P N to the right and left; also extend sides K P and T N; make P C and N B equal heights P C and N B at Fig. 2; draw from C through B, cutting at V; make N L equal N P; join L B. This gives L B C for the pitches of tangents on lower wreath piece. To find the angle which these tangents make on the surface of mould. This is done by drawing from N square with B C; take B as centre and L radius; draw the circle, cutting line from N at A; join it and B. This gives A B C as the angle.

We must now find pitch of plank, and half the long diameter of a semi-ellipse, in order to strike curves on mould with a string. To do this, draw from V through T; draw from P parallel with T V; again draw through K square with T V, cutting at 2 J; make P 3 equal 2 J; join 3 C. This is pitch of plank. Now make P R equal P N; square up from R, cutting at D. This gives D C as half long diameter of semi-ellipse. The position of short diameter on the long, is found by making P E equal K J; square up from E, cutting at F, which gives F C; this done, set a rule to angle A B C. Be correct in this; now lift the rule and lay it on a piece of board, shown at Fig. 4; mark A B C; extend B A; make A 3 equal A 3 at the ramp below; draw joints through 3 and C square with tangents. This done,

come to Fig. 3, and take P J as radius; return with it to joint C as centre; draw the arc at F; come again to same place, and take 2 T as radius; return with it to A as centre; draw the arc. Now draw a line touching both arcs, and we have the position of long diameter; draw from C square with long diameter, cutting at F; make F L equal F C above Fig. 3 on the right; now make L J equal D C at the place just mentioned; square up a line from L; make L O equal one side of square, Fig. 3; set off on each side of O half width of rail.

The width of mould at each end is obtained as usual by finding bevels for joints. This is done at any convenient place, say Fig. 5. Here draw two lines any distance apart, but parallel with long diameter at the mould; take any point on lower line as V; square up from it, cutting at N. This done, come to C at upper part of plate; take it as centre, and with any radius draw the arc O O'; return with it to V as centre, and draw arc O O'; make both arcs measure equal; draw through V and O, cutting at P; draw P R parallel with A B on mould; take N as centre, and for radius a circle touching P R, cutting at C; draw from it through V. This gives bevel W for joint at 3 on the mould. Draw from P a line parallel with A L on mould; take N again as centre, and for radius a circle touching line just drawn from P, the circle cutting at S; draw through it and V. This gives bevel X for joint at C on mould. The application of both bevels to joints, is shown by the square sections on right and left.

To find width of mould at each joint, set off half width of rail below V; draw it parallel with V O', cutting bevel lines, which gives K V to set off on each side of 3 at the joint, and E V to set off on each side of C at joint on the right. Then 2 V, being set off on each side of J on long diameter, gives width of elliptic curves, by means of which, and width of rail on short diameter, we find points for pins, in order to sweep the curves with a string. This being done, the mould for lower wreath piece is complete.

Fig. 6. To draw a mould for upper wreath piece. This is a simple affair, and quickly done by laying the framing square on a piece of board, and drawing the right angle C D 2; make C D equal the pitch C D, Fig. 2; square down from C, and make C E equal N P on plan; draw through E parallel with C D; set off half width of rail on each side of C. To find width of mould on wide end and a bevel for joint. This is done by making E N equal E D at Fig. 2; draw from N through C, which gives bevel L for joint. Now draw the line, cutting at K, and we have C K to set off on each side of 2 at the joint. The width being obtained, draw straight wood parallel with 2 D, the length of this four or five inches. Now find points for pins, and sweep the curves with a string, which completes the mould.

Here, remember, it has already been stated, that the application of all moulds is simple, yet positive. The rule perhaps had better be repeated, which is as follows: The wreath piece having been cut square through the plank, and joints made, then the bevel is applied. Its stock rests on the surface, and its blade passing through a point which is in half the width and half thickness of stuff; the line made by bevel is to be continued on both surfaces and square with joint. Then, similar lines being on both surfaces of mould, these lines, and those on the piece, are made to fall directly over each other, so that the exact cylinder form of a wreath is given by a mould being applied in the manner just stated. The same rule holds good for the thickness, half of which always passes through half the thickness of plank. Adhere to these plain and simple directions, and no errors or mistakes can possibly occur in forming a wreath.

144

Plate 48.

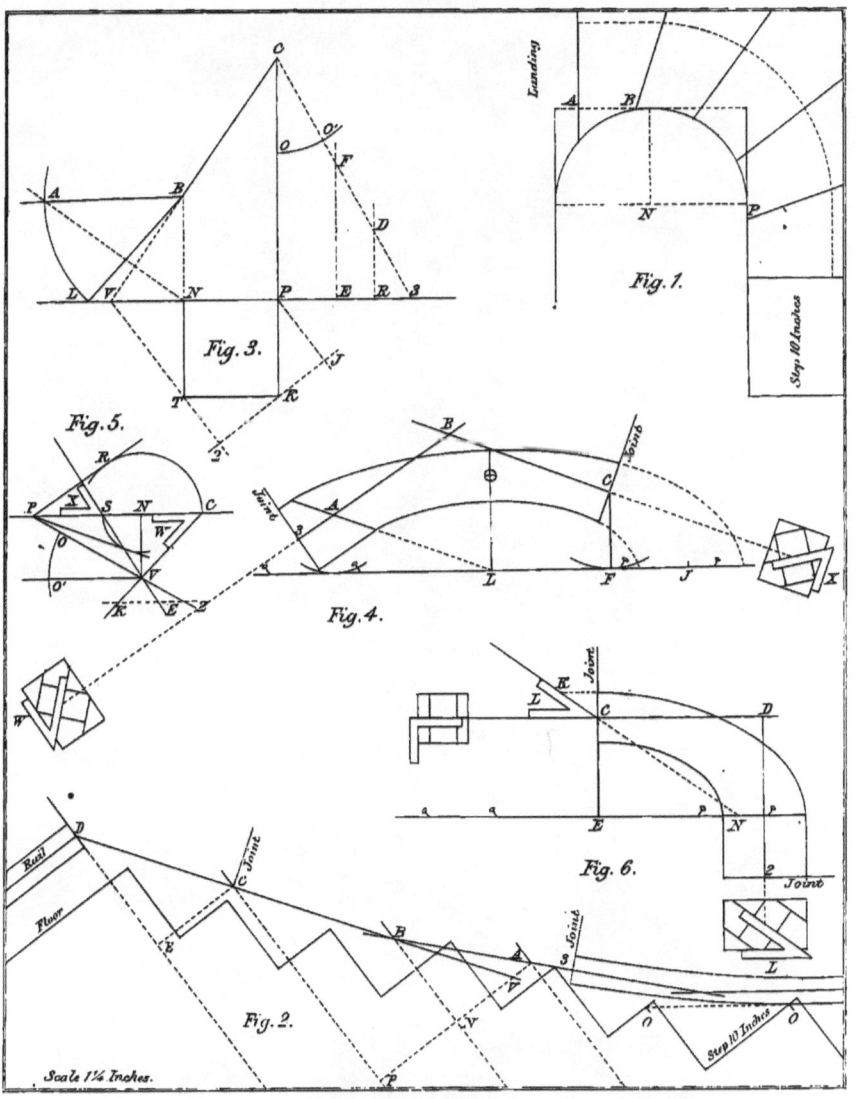

Fig.1.

Fig.3.

Fig.5.

Fig.4.

Fig.6.

Fig.2.

Scale 1¼ Inches.

Step 10 Inches.

Step 10 Inches.

www.ingramcontent.com/pod-product-compliance
Lightning Source LLC
Chambersburg PA
CBHW030904050726
47500CB00009B/1014